Fairy Tales from Around the World

70 TINY NIGHTTIME TALES

Illustrations by Anna Láng

STERLING CHILDREN'S BOOKS
New York

Contents

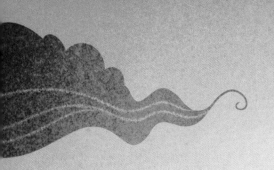

Introduction

"Will you tell me a story?"

Every evening at bedtime, children around the world ask to be told a story. It's part of a ritual that helps them relax into a peaceful night's sleep.

Fairy tales and fables are perfect for this, leading children on an adventure full of unforgettable characters, emotions, and magic, yet also helping soothe and calm them.

The tales in this book are no exception, and they have another benefit: They can all be read in five minutes, making it easy to fit story time in at the end of a busy day.

A Pot of Gold

There was once a wise peasant who lived in a mountain village with his three sons. The boys lounged about all day long, doing nothing from morning to evening while their father worked hard from sunrise to sunset. But one day, sadly, the peasant got sick. While he was stuck in bed, his land was so neglected that it became frighteningly barren and wild.

"What ever will we do?" cried one of the boys.

"Who will farm the land?" said another, worried.

"How will we get enough to eat?" yelled the third out of despair.

The peasant gathered his three sons around his bed and told them a secret: He had buried a pot of gold on the land.

"Look for it carefully on our property. Dig up every inch, and you'll be rich!"

Naturally, the three boys ran outside and began to dig. They dug, and they dug, and they dug some more until they'd gone through the entire the field, but they didn't find the pot of gold.

"Well, let's plant some crops!" suggested the second brother.

And with that, they planted, watered, and harvested wheat.

"Why don't we sell some of our harvest at the market?" asked the youngest brother.

Their effort earned them a lot of money, and finally they understood their father's lesson: "So that's what he wanted to teach us! Only with hard work and lots of effort do you earn something precious."

From that day on, the three brothers rolled up their sleeves and become great farmers, just like their father.

Puss in Boots

An old miller left all his property to his sons: The eldest got the mill and the middle son got the donkey, but the third only got the cat. Seeing the disappointment of his young owner, the cat began to talk. "I can make you rich," the cat said. "Trust me. All I need is a sack and a pair of boots."

Once he had the requested items, the cat pulled on the boots and put a moorhen in the sack, which he took to the king as a gift from the Marquis of Carabas. The king thanked him and asked him about his mysterious owner. Puss in Boots talked for hours about the marquis' wealth and riches. Then, he bowed to the king and went on his way.

A few days later, the king went on a carriage ride with his daughter. The cat was waiting for them. He stopped the carriage and asked for help.

"The Marquis of Carabas has been robbed and thrown in the river! Your Majesty, can you help him and let him aboard your carriage?"

The king, curious to meet the noble he had heard so much about, gladly agreed. Little did he know, the "marquis" was the cat's owner, who the cat had convinced to dive into the river. Still, the marquis was so charming and mysterious that he made quite an impression on the princess. Likewise, the young man was enchanted by her beauty.

The cat then suggested that they all dine at the marquis' palace, winking at his astonished owner. He scampered off to the castle of the horrible local ogre, getting there before everyone else. When he got to the drawbridge, a scary voice greeted him. It was the ogre!

"Who are you? And how dare you enter my castle? You'll pay, with your life!"

The cat wasn't intimidated and answered defiantly: "They say you're a great wizard, but I bet you can't even turn yourself into something small and tiny, like a mouse."

"Ha ha ha," laughed the ogre, "that's child's play!"

In a snap, the ogre turned into a mouse. Equally as fast, Puss in Boots pounced and devoured him in one mouthful.

Just then, the king's carriage arrived, and the cat rushed to welcome it.

"Welcome to the palace of the Marquis of Carabas!"

The king, impressed by the elegance and riches of the castle and won over by the personality of the young miller his daughter had fallen in love with, happily approved of the marriage between the two.

And Puss in Boots? He took those uncomfortable boots off and, from that day on, spent his days lazing about the castle, curled up on soft pillows and enjoying bowls of milk!

The Frog Prince

There was once a princess who was so beautiful that even the sun was in awe of her. When it was hot, she would go to the woods to cool down at a pond under an old linden tree. If she got bored, she'd play with a golden ball. It was her favorite toy!

One day the ball disappeared into the water. The princess began to cry.

A voice called out to her. "What's wrong, young princess?"

Shocked, the princess looked around for the source of the voice. "Oh! It's you, frog!" the princess said. "I'm crying because my golden ball fell into the pond."

"Don't cry! I can help you, but what will you give me in return?" the frog said.

"Whatever you want, dear frog! Clothes, gold, jewels?" she asked.

"I just want to be your friend, to play with you, eat from your plate, and sleep in your bed," replied the frog.

"Alright. Just bring my ball back," she replied.

The frog dove in and threw the ball up onto the grass. Overjoyed, the princess ran off.

"Wait, princess! You must carry me. I can't run that fast," yelled the frog.

But the young maiden didn't hear him and soon forgot all about him.

The next day, someone knocked on the door while the princess was eating lunch with her father.

"Princess, open up!" said a hoarse voice.

It was the frog! The princess slammed the door and sat back down, shaking with fright.

"What's wrong, my dear?" asked the king.

"The ugly frog who helped me retrieve my lost ball from the pond is outside. I promised him I'd bring him with me everywhere!"

"Promises are meant to be kept!" the king said. "Let him in."

The frog was invited to lunch, where he ate from the princess's plate. "I've eaten enough. Now I'm tired and I want to take a nap!"

The princess burst into tears. She didn't want to even touch the frog. But the king scolded her again, reminding her that we mustn't scorn those who help us when we're in need.

When they got to her room, the frog set up his pillow next to the princess, who was horrified at the idea of having to spend the night next to her unwelcome guest.

The following morning, the frog asked the girl for a kiss. In exchange, he promised to disappear from her life forever.

Overcoming her disgust for the creature, the princess took him in her hands and gave him a little kiss. Magically, the frog turned into a handsome prince.
He explained that a spiteful sorceress had put a spell on him. Only the kiss of a princess could break the spell. The young prince asked the princess if she would marry him, and the princess agreed.

The next morning, eight white horses with plumes of feathers on their bridles took the two young lovebirds to the prince's castle, where they lived happily ever after.

Grandfather's glove

On a cold, snowy day, a grandfather lost his glove as he walked through a forest with his cart.

A little mouse found it and happily thought: "I've found a warm place to stay for the winter!" And he squeezed himself into the glove.

After a little while, a frog came along. "Who lives here?" he asked.

"A mouse! And who are you?"

"I'm a frog. Can I come in?" he replied.

"Yes, come in!" said the rodent.

Later, a little rabbit came along. The rabbit stopped and timidly asked, "Who lives here?"

"A little mouse and a frog. Who are you?" the two animals answered in unison.

"I'm a bunny! Can I please come in and warm up?"

"Okay, come on in and join us," said his two new friends.

Along came a fox, who asked who lived in the glove. Even she joined them!

Soon, a wolf and a boar arrived. When they squeezed their way into the glove, it was such a tight fit that no one could move!

Then a bear appeared. "Who lives here?" asked the bear in a deep, deep voice.

"A mouse, a frog, a rabbit, a fox, a boar, and a wolf," the animals replied.

"But . . . how did you all fit?" said the bear.

"Who are you, anyway?"

"I'm a bear! Come on, let me in!"

"But, how? There's no more room!"

"Just scoot over!"

"All right, but promise you'll stay in a corner."

And just like that, the glove became the home of seven animals! It was so full it looked like a blown up balloon. In the meantime, the grandfather realized he had lost his glove and went back to look for it. When he found it, he saw that it was moving about quite strangely. His dog even started barking: "Woof! Woof! Woof!"

The grandfather couldn't believe his eyes. Looking closer, he saw the head of the mouse, the tail of the fox, the tip of a rabbit's ear, a bit of fur and sharp, shiny teeth! Frightened by the old man, the animals all hopped out of the glove and ran into the woods. The grandfather, on the other hand, grabbed his glove and went home!

The Wild Swans

Once upon a time, there was a king who had eleven sons and one daughter. His beloved queen had died, and he decided to remarry. Little did he know, the woman he chose as his wife was a witch!

The new queen managed to hide her wicked ways from the king, but the princes uncovered her true nature. Hoping to keep her secret, the queen found a way to send all of the children to live far, far away. The princess was sent to be a maid in a distant castle. After she left, the queen turned the boys into eleven swans who could only return to human form for a few hours each night.

A year later, the young princess returned to the castle. When her brothers didn't come to greet her, the princess was filled with despair. She wandered the forests, mountains, and plains for days.

Eventually, she came upon a nice old witch's house. The princess called to her: "Kind woman, have you seen eleven boys pass by? They're my brothers and I haven't had any news of them in a long time."

The old woman answered, "I have not, but there are eleven beautiful swans that live in a pond not far from here."

The princess walked to the pond and watched the swans as she thought about her brothers' fate. It soon grew dark and before her incredulous eyes, the eleven swans transformed into her eleven brothers. The children hugged each other, delighting in their reunion. The boys told their sister about the curse that their evil stepmother had put on them to keep them from their father.

The young princess then went and asked the good witch for help. She didn't have the power to break the curse, but she could help the girl.

"The only way to break the curse is to find the enchanted field, not far from here, collect some thistles, spin them, and weave them into shirts for your brothers to wear. Be careful though! You mustn't tell anyone!" she said.

The girl went straight to the enchanted field and began collecting thistles, continuing even as their spikes injured her hands.

One day, while the young princess was hard at work, a handsome prince approached. The pair fell madly in love and he brought her to his castle. The prince and princess got married, but she never stopped spinning the thistles to break the cruel spell that had been cast on her brothers.

Unfortunately, the prince's mother was also a wicked witch. She decided to make the princess's life very, very difficult. When the prince set off on a long journey, the princess gave birth to two sweet twins. Her mother-in-law transformed the twins into two scary spiders and accused the princess of a terrible crime: "You're an evil witch and you did this with the magic of your thistles!"

She demanded that the princess be burned at the stake before the entire town. But even during her imprisonment, the princess never stopped weaving shirts with the thread made from the thistles.

Execution day arrived. The princess stood on the giant pile of wood. The fire was about to be lit when the princess heard the beating of eleven pairs of wings. As the swans drew near, the princess quickly threw the shirts she had made onto each of them, and the swans turned into men. Unfortunately, one of the shirts was still missing a sleeve, and the youngest brother had one wing instead of an arm.

Finally reunited, the brothers told their story and freed the princess. Together, the brothers and sister made her wicked mother-in-law turn the twins back into human children before forcing her into exile. The brothers returned to their home and drove out their evil stepmother, bringing peace and justice to their kingdom.

And the princess? She lived happily ever after with her husband and their children.

The Ugly Duckling

One beautiful summer day, a mama duck waited patiently for her eggs to hatch. Soon, there were lots of lively little ducklings out and about, looking around with wonder. But one egg, the biggest one, still hadn't hatched. Mama duck sat and warmed it a little while longer. Finally, it cracked open, and out popped a baby bird that seemed too large to be a duckling!

"Could it be a turkey?" thought the worried mama duck.

She gathered up her ducklings and led them to the canal. She jumped in the water, followed by her offspring who dived in without fear. They reemerged in a second, with even the youngest swimming effortlessly. That reassured mama duck. No turkey could swim that well!

After their dip in the water, they returned to the banks and headed for the coop. There they met up with other mama ducks and ducklings. The new arrivals aroused a lot of curiosity, but the youngest, biggest one got some very mean comments.

"He's gigantic! And ugly, too!" they said, laughing.

Mama duck gave him a hug and reassured him, but no one wanted to play with the large duckling. After a while, the poor thing grew sad and lonely.

Days passed, and even his own brothers and sisters began avoiding him. So, the ugly duckling decided to run away.

He ventured far from the roost, reaching a big, expansive swamp where wild ducks lived. But he wasn't any better off; it was hunting season and the area wasn't safe.

The ugly duckling continued searching for a place where he could live happily and be accepted for who he was. No matter where he went, he was mocked for being awkward and clumsy. He spent most of his time alone.

One fall evening, the duck saw a flock of beautiful white birds take flight. They had big, broad wings and long, flexible necks. Oh how he wished to be graceful like them!

Winter was long and lonely, but finally spring arrived. The duckling had changed with the weather: His wings were stronger, sturdier, and supported his weight effortlessly.

Later that spring, three beautiful white swans landed in the canal near him, swimming elegantly through the water. The duckling decided to join them, hoping not to be chased away. He flew over to them, expecting the worst. As he lowered his gaze to the surface of the water, he caught sight of his reflection. He was no longer an ungainly, ugly duckling. He was a magnificent swan!

The other swans swam toward him and as they approached, they caressed him with their beaks to welcome him. He had finally found his place in the world, and no one would ever mock him again!

Sleeping Beauty

One spring, many years ago, a king and a queen were delighted at the birth of their beautiful baby girl. To celebrate her birth, the couple decided to hold a grand christening. The king invited seven fairies in his kingdom, but forgot to include the old fairy of the mountain who lived alone in her cave and spent her time studying witchcraft.

During the party, each guest approached the princess to present the gifts they had brought her. Finally, the seven fairy godmothers came to her crib and gave the girl gifts that would serve her well throughout her life. They granted her the gifts of beauty, wit, grace, song, dance, and kindness.

As the last fairy was about to offer the princess the gift of happiness, a gust of wind blew open the doors of the castle and the mountain witch appeared in the center of a thick, black cloud of smoke, furious that she wasn't invited.

"I'm a much more powerful sorceress than any fairy, and I won't stand to be ignored!" she said.

"I'm sorry if I have offended you," said the king. "I hope you can forgive us."

"Of course, your Majesty, but only if I too can give a gift to the princess."

The king agreed, relieved that they had not made an enemy of the powerful fairy. And then she revealed her gift: "When the princess turns eighteen years old, she will prick her finger with a spindle and die!"

With that, the mountain witch disappeared, leaving the king and queen in tears.

But the princess had not been granted her final gift. The youngest fairy, who had

been interrupted by the witch, said, "My powers aren't strong enough to stop the curse, but I can use my gift to lessen it. Sleeping Beauty will prick her finger, but she won't die. Instead, she and the entire court will sleep for one hundred years. Only the kiss of her true love will be able to wake her."

The king and queen, despite feeling a bit relieved, ordered all spindles in the kingdom to be burned.

Years passed, and the princess grew into a beautiful, kind, and happy young woman.

As the royal court was getting ready to celebrate the princess's eighteenth birthday, she grew bored and decided to admire the view from the highest point of the tower. Once she got to the top of the stairs, she saw an old woman spinning thread in a small room.

"What is that?" asked the princess.

"It's a spindle, princess. Would you like to try?"

The princess took the offered spindle and immediately pricked her finger. Suddenly she felt very, very tired. The last thing the princess heard was the old woman's

laughter as the mountain witch's curse took effect. The princess and the royal court fell into a deep sleep and the castle was enveloped by an impenetrable forest of brambles.

As time passed, the legend of Sleeping Beauty spread through the land, but no one was ever able to get through the forest.

One day, a prince arrived in the kingdom. During his travels, he had heard whispers of the enchanted castle and decided to search for it. As he approached the bramble bush, the sun rose and marked one hundred years since the beginning of the princess's curse, ending the spell that kept the castle hidden. The brambles turned to beautiful flowers that moved out of the Prince's way as he passed.

The prince reached the castle easily. He walked through the great halls where all the court slept, and continued on to the room at the top of the tower. There he found the princess, sound asleep. Entranced by her beauty, he walked over to her and gave her a kiss. Suddenly, she blinked and opened her eyes, waking up from her deep sleep — and with her, the entire royal court. A magnificent party was held to celebrate the end of the spell and the marriage of the young prince and princess.

Frau Holle

There was once a widow who had two daughters. One was pretty and industrious. The other—her favorite—was ugly and lazy. The first one had to do the worst chores, spinning yarn until her fingers bled. One day, the reel slipped out of her hand and fell into the well where she was trying to clean her wounds. Crying, she ran to her stepmother, who scolded her. "You dropped the reel, now go fish it out of the water!"

The young girl went back to the well and jumped in. She fainted, but when she awoke she was in a flowery meadow. As she explored, she found an oven filled with bread. The bread called out to her.

"Take me out, or I'll burn!" it said. So, she did just that.

She kept walking until she came to a tree full of apples. The tree yelled, "Shake me! My apples are all ripe."

The young girl shook the tree until all the apples fell to the ground, then continued on her way.

Finally, she came to a cottage that housed an old woman with long, sharp teeth. The old woman greeted her. "Don't be afraid. I am Frau Holle. Stay here with me. If you do my housework well, you will be well rewarded. You must make my bed carefully, and shake it diligently until the feathers fly. Then it will snow in the world."

The girl agreed and stayed with Frau Holle for some time. Frau Holle treated her well and the girl was at peace, though she missed home terribly. She told the old woman, who replied, "I understand. Because you have served me so faithfully, I'll accompany you back home myself."

Frau Holle led her to a big door, where it began to rain gold, covering her entirely. "Go on, you deserve it," said Frau Holle as she gave her the reel that had fallen into the well.

The door closed and the girl found herself just outside her home. As soon as she entered the courtyard, the rooster crowed:

"Cock-a-doodle-doo! Our golden girl is here anew!"

When the girl walked into the house covered in gold, her stepmother wanted to know

how she had earned such riches. After listening to her, the stepmother decided that her other daughter should have the same opportunity. So, the lazy sister sat down to spin, dropped her reel into the well, and jumped in to fetch it. Like her sister, she awoke in a meadow full of flowers and headed down the trail. When she reached the oven, however, she ignored the pleas of the bread and did the same at the apple tree. Finally, she reached Frau Holle and began working for her.

The first day she forced herself to be industrious, but gradually she became lazier and lazier. She got up late, she made the bed poorly, and she didn't shake it until the feathers flew. The old woman soon grew tired of such behavior and fired her. Frau Holle escorted the girl to the door, but when the lazy sister stood under it, she was doused with tar instead of gold. "That's the reward you deserve," said Frau Holle as she closed the door.

The lazy sister returned home covered in tar, which she was unable to remove for the rest of her life. When he saw her, the rooster crowed:

"Cock-a-doodle-doo! Our dirty girl is here anew!"

The Town Musicians of Bremen

A donkey that had spent its entire life pulling a cart decided to run away when his owner said he was getting too old to do the job. "I'll go to Bremen! It's a city full of artists, and I'll finally be able to fulfill my dream of becoming a musician." Along the way, he passed an old dog that had stopped to catch his breath.

"Why are you panting so hard? Where are you going?" asked the donkey.

"I don't know. I just want to get away from my master. He thinks I'm too old to work and he wanted to get rid of me," answered the dog.

"Come with me to Bremen. We'll make a living as musicians!"

Farther down the road, they came across a cat and a rooster. The cat wasn't much of a mouse-hunter any more, and the rooster had been crowing late these days. All four agreed that Bremen was the place for them. They continued on down the road, singing as they walked.

A few hours passed, but Bremen was still far away. The animals, tired and hungry, decided to stop at a house that gave off the delicious smell of roasting food. Trying

not to make noise, they crept up to the window and peeked inside, holding their breath so they wouldn't get caught. The table was set with bread, lots of cheese, ham, and an enormous berry pie, but there were four thieves enjoying the feast!

"We could ask them to host us," said the rooster hesitantly.

"Are you kidding?" barked the dog. "I know those guys! I've chased them off my master's land hundreds of times. But now I'm old and I wouldn't even be able to bite their legs!"

The cat, however, had an idea. She asked the donkey to quietly rest his hooves on the windowsill. Then, the dog hopped onto the the donkey's back, the cat climbed up to sit on the dog's head, and the rooster perched on the cat's shoulders. When the donkey nodded, the musicians began their first concert! The cat meowed, the donkey brayed, the dog barked, and the rooster made such a noise that the thieves ran for their lives. Without missing a beat, the four friends walked into the house and sat around the table. Some say they are still there, enjoying their feast!

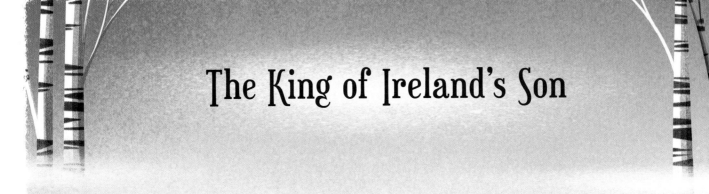

The King of Ireland's Son

One winter day, as the King of Ireland's eldest son was walking through the snow-covered woods, he pricked his finger on a blackberry bush. A few drops of his blood fell on the white snow near a raven's fallen feather. The prince immediately promised himself that one day, he would marry a girl with hair as black as a raven's wings, skin as white as snow, and lips as red as blood. He began a journey to search for her.

In a faraway village, he met a family mourning their father's death. They were so poor that they couldn't afford a decent funeral, so the young prince paid for it.

Soon after, he saved a gnome that was being threatened by a giant bird of prey. The gnome offered himself to his service, asking for the first kiss of the prince's future wife in return. The prince agreed.

During their travels, they encountered a hunter, armed with a rifle. The gnome suggested the prince hire the hunter to his service and offer a plot of land in exchange. The prince agreed.

A little farther, they met a man lying with his ear to the ground. Once again, the gnome suggested the prince hire him in exchange for a piece of land and once again, the prince agreed.

Continuing on, they met a man who could make the blades of a windmill turn just by blowing on them. The gnome offered his usual suggestion to the prince, who agreed.

Finally, they came across a man who was able to split wood with just his foot. And once again, the prince agreed to hire him for their journey, and promised a piece of land in return.

The group soon came to a village with a menacing castle that towered over it. They asked the townspeople about the castle, and they responded that it belonged to a giant who had locked up a beautiful princess with skin as white as snow, hair as black as a raven, and lips as red as blood.

The prince walked up to the door of the castle and knocked, determined to save the princess. The giant answered. "You can have the princess only if you can pass my tests. Otherwise, you'll die!"

The giant brought him to three constantly moving targets and said the prince would have to hit them all perfectly in the center. The hunter stepped forward and easily accomplished the feat.

Then, the giant said, "Lie down on the ground and tell me what the ants are saying!" The man that they had found with his ear to the ground reported the ants' every word.

Next, the giant said, "Sow all these seeds with just one breath!" The man whose breath turned the blades of a windmill completed the job.

The giant took the prince to the woods and yelled, "Cut down all these trees in half an hour!" The man who could cut wood with just one foot completed the task in no time at all.

The giant had no choice but to give up. He said, "You win. You can go kiss the princess!" But the gnome reminded the prince of his promise—that the gnome would get to kiss his future bride. So, the gnome went to the young lady, who was seated on a beautiful throne, surrounded by venomous snakes. The gnome got rid of all the snakes and then had the prince enter the room.

"Thank you for helping me," said the prince.

The gnome replied, "It is I who should thank you. I'm the gnome protector of the family who you helped by paying for their father's funeral, and I wanted to repay you for your generosity."

The Prince of Ireland returned home with his princess. The couple married and lived happily ever after with their new gnome protector.

Aladdin

There was once a rebellious, stubborn young man named Aladdin who lived in an Arabian city. One day, while strolling about the bazaar, Aladdin bumped into a famous magician who claimed to be his uncle. The magician asked Aladdin to help him complete a task in Spirit Mountain, promising that they would return with great riches.

After a day of travel, the two reached the base of a mountain, which held the entrance to a cave.

As they approached the entrance, the magician said, "Aladdin, go into the cave and bring me the lamp that you'll find hidden in a small hole on the wall."

Aladdin entered, found the lamp, and brought it to the mouth of the cave, where the magician was waiting for him.

"Give me the lamp!" the magician said impatiently.

"I'll give it to you once I get out of here," Aladdin replied.

Angered, the magician rolled large stones toward Aladdin, hoping to grab the lamp before the young man fell back into the cave, but Aladdin took the lamp with him.

He found himself in the pitch black. In attempt to get some light, he rubbed the old lamp. To his surprise, a genie emerged from it. The genie said, "You've freed me from my prison. You are now my master, and your wish is my command."

So, Aladdin ordered, "Take me home at once!"

The words had barely left his lips when the earth opened up. Flying in the arms of the genie, Aladdin was in front of his home in a matter of seconds.

One morning, while at the bazaar, Aladdin saw the sultan's daughter, escorted by the royal guards. He instantly fell in love with her and knew he had to see her again. He asked the genie to give him a flying carpet that could take him to the princess's room at the top of the highest tower of the royal palace. When he got there, the princess was fascinated by the carpet. She asked Aladdin to take her on a trip to see the world. They flew all night.

Upon their return, Aladdin went to the sultan and said, "Your majesty, I am in love with your daughter. May I have her hand in marriage?"

The sultan laughed. "You can marry her only if you can build her a worthy palace within the next three days!"

Aladdin asked the genie to help him. In three hours, a magnificent palace was completed. The sultan had no choice but to let Aladdin marry his daughter.

The tale of the incredible event soon reached the magician, who decided it was time to get hold of the lamp that had once eluded him.

The magician pretended to be a dealer of rare goods and went to the palace while Aladdin was away. There, he convinced the princess to give him the old lamp in exchange for a new one. When he had the lamp in his hands, he called upon the genie.

"Take me, the princess, and the entire palace far from here!"

The genie was furious, but he was required to obey the owner of the lamp.

When Aladdin returned to the palace and realized what had happened, he hopped on the flying carpet and took off. In a few hours he reached the place where the palace was now standing and got the lamp back. The genie was quite happy to see his young master. Aladdin ordered the genie to take him and the princess home, and to leave the magician in the cave where Aladdin had been trapped.

The genie obeyed and prepared to return to his lamp. Aladdin stopped him.

"I have one last wish for you," he said. "I want the curse of the lamp to be lifted and for you to be free to go where you please and do what your heart desires."

The genie, happy at last, flew all the way to the stars, free for the first time in thousands of years.

The Nightingale

In the forest that surrounded the Chinese emperor's palace lived a nightingale whose melodic song drew travelers from every corner of the Earth. When word of the bird reached the emperor, he demanded that it be brought to his court immediately.

That evening, the nightingale sang so beautifully that the ruler was moved to tears. He decided that the bird would stay with him, forever locked in a golden cage.

One day, a mechanical nightingale covered in gold and precious gems was brought to the royal palace. As soon as it was wound, it began to sing.

The emperor wanted the two birds, the real one and the mechanical one, to compete to see which sang best.

Both were wonderful, but the people loved the mechanical bird more because it was also very beautiful. It sang the same song thirty-three times in a row. Even though the people would have happily listened to its call again, the emperor decided he wanted to hear the real nightingale. But while the crowd had been distracted by the mechanical bird, the real one had flown away.

After their initial shock, everyone agreed that the mechanical nightingale was much better anyway. The real nightingale was banned from the empire, and the mechanical bird was placed on a silk pillow near the emperor's bed.

One evening, the mechanical bird made a strange grinding noise and the music stopped. The emperor called the watchmaker to fix it. Once the mechanical bird was repaired, the watchmaker said the emperor must use it very carefully, as the gears inside were worn out.

Over the years, the emperor's health declined. One evening, his servants found him so pale and cold in bed that they thought he was dead!

Yet the emperor was still alive. He was having trouble breathing and saw Death himself, wearing the emperor's splendid crown, and holding a gold sword in one hand and a beautiful banner in the other.

The emperor managed to whisper, "I want music! Beloved golden nightingale, sing as loudly as you can!"

The nightingale stayed silent because no one was there to wind him.

Just then, from the window, the emperor heard a beautiful song. The small, wild nightingale had come to comfort the king with its melodies. As the bird sang, the emperor began to feel better and regain his strength.

Even Death began to listen, urging the nightingale not to stop. "Go on, little nightingale. Keep singing!" he said.

"Only if you give me your gold sword and luxurious banner, and hand over the emperor's crown!" the nightingale said.

Without hesitating, Death gave the nightingale all that he had asked for. The nightingale sang of a peaceful cemetery where white roses bloomed and the sweet smell of an elder tree filled the air. The song reminded Death of his garden. Filled with nostalgia, he flew away.

The emperor thanked the nightingale a thousand times.

"My little friend, I imprisoned you and then banished you from my kingdom. Yet you still came to my rescue. How can I repay you?" he said.

"You've already repaid me," replied the bird. "I shall never forget your tears the first time I sang for you. For now, get well. I will sing for you again."

The next morning, the emperor woke up healed and full of energy.

"Stay with me forever!" he said to the nightingale. "Sing only when you want to and I'll destroy that mechanical bird!"

"Don't do it!" said the nightingale. "Keep it with you, as I cannot live in the palace. I'll still come every night and sing for you, so that you can relax and think about all the good you can do for those who are suffering and how you'll fix the injustices that happen without your knowledge. But you have to promise me something."

"Anything," the emperor replied.

"You mustn't tell anyone that I'm the one to report what is happening in your kingdom." And with that, the nightingale flew away.

The Prince Who Married a Frog

A wise king that lived in a far away kingdom didn't want his three sons to become rivals when searching for their future wives. He told his sons to aim their slingshots in different directions, shoot a stone, and propose to the girls who were closest to their stones' landing places.

The three princes obeyed their father. The oldest one found the daughter of a baker next to his stone, the second a weaver, and the third . . . a frog!

The king decided that he would leave his kingdom to the son who had found the best bride. He gave each prince some hemp fibers, instructing them to return it spun into thread within three days.

On that day, the frog gave the prince a walnut while the weaver delivered perfectly spun thread. You can surely imagine how the young prince felt when he appeared before his father with a walnut!

But as soon as the king opened the shell, out came masterfully spun cloth, fine as silk and so big it filled the entire throne room.

While the king was quite impressed, he simply couldn't have a frog inherit his kingdom, so he gave his sons a new test. The king's favorite hunting hound had just had puppies. He gave one to each of his sons and said that the girl who took the best care of her dog would become queen.

A few months passed and the three brides appeared before the king with the dogs. The baker girl arrived with a giant robust mastiff; the weaver a ferocious hound. The frog, however, gave the king a box. The king was perplexed, but when he opened it, he found a tiny poodle who could do tricks and flips, and even count!

In that very moment, the king decided that his youngest son and the frog would inherit the throne, and all of the princes were set to marry on the same day.

The big day finally arrived, and the two older brothers went to fetch their brides with carriages adorned with flowers and scented garlands. The two young ladies were beautiful in their magnificent white dresses.

The youngest prince looked for his frog and found her near a ditch on a carriage made of a fig leaf, pulled by four snails. The prince set off, but snails are very slow and the young man soon had to stop to wait for his fiancée to catch up. He fell asleep as he waited. When he awoke, he saw before him a golden carriage upholstered in exquisite velvet. Inside, a beautiful young lady awaited him, wearing a marvelous emerald green dress.

"Who are you?" asked the prince.

"I'm your frog," she responded.

"You can't be!" said the prince.

In response, she opened a small chest and pulled out a fig leaf, the shells of four snails, and the skin of a frog.

"Once, I was a princess, but a wicked spell turned me into a frog and condemned me to remain that way until a prince agreed to marry me."

Overjoyed, the prince introduced her to his father, who was also very happy to know that a frog would not take the throne after all!

Rapunzel

There was once a couple who awaited the arrival of their first child. Every day, the mother-to-be looked out of the window to admire the vegetable patch of the witch who lived next door. She had never seen such delicious looking vegetables. The thing she most wanted were the wonderful rapunzel roots, which are similar to parsnips. She wanted to eat them so badly that she stopped eating anything else and fell ill. Worried, her husband asked what he could do.

"I absolutely must try the rapunzel from the witch's garden," she replied.

One night, her husband snuck into the vegetable patch and took a single rapunzel root. As he turned to leave, he heard the old witch cry, "What are you doing? Why are you stealing my rapunzel?"

"It's for my wife," explained the man. "She's pregnant and it's all she wants to eat!"

The witch said, "Fine you can have them. But when your child is born, you must give her to me!"

The man agreed, comforted by the idea that the girl would grow up next door. When he handed her over, the witch disappeared, taking little Rapunzel with her to the woods. She hid the girl in a doorless tower that was built with magic.

Years passed and the girl grew, as did her hair, which no one bothered to cut. Each day, the witch visited the tower and yelled out, "Rapunzel, Rapunzel, let down your hair!" The girl would lower her long braids out of the window, which the witch used to scale the tower.

One day, a prince witnessed this. Once the witch left, he stood under the tower and said, "Rapunzel, Rapunzel, let down your hair!" She was a bit frightened when she saw the prince climb through the window, but before long the two fell in love.

The prince visited Rapunzel in secret, until one day, the witch saw him descend from the tower and was filled with rage. She cut Rapunzel's long hair and locked her in a cave before blinding the prince with a spell. He wandered desparately around the woods until he heard a voice singing in the distance.

The prince followed the voice to a cave and moved the boulder blocking the entrance. Rapunzel rushed out. The couple embraced, Rapunzel so happy that she cried tears of joy. Two of those tears fell on the prince's eyes and broke the evil spell. Now that they had found each other, nothing could separate them. The witch was never seen again.

Spriditis

There once was a man named Spriditis who was very little but also very brave.

One day, he decided to leave his hometown and see the world.

When night fell, he stopped to sleep under a tree in the woods. A squire walked by as he slept. It was dark and the squire almost stepped right on Spriditis. Luckily, the squire stopped in time. He exclaimed, "Little Frog, what are you doing in the woods at night?"

Spriditis was very tired, and he didn't wake up. The squire called his men and ordered them all to fire a shot together. Even that ruckus didn't wake Spriditis.

The squire ordered them to shoot again, but still nothing.

"Shoot!" he yelled a third time.

With that, Spriditis woke and jumped up angrily. He yelled, "You better watch out! If I hit you, you're in real trouble!"

The squire burst into laughter.

"Can you even fight a grasshopper?" he said.

"I could fight a bear! And if you don't believe me, bring me one and you'll see. Then I bet you'd be so impressed, you'd want me as your son-in-law!" said Spriditis.

"Fine," said the squire. "If you can beat a bear, I'll give you my daughter's hand in marriage. But if you fail, you'll get a beating!"

At dawn, a giant bear began to approach but ran away as soon as it saw the hunters. Spriditis filled his pockets with pebbles and chased after it.

When he caught up to the bear, it was sleeping near a hay barn. Spriditis threw one of the pebbles at it. The bear woke up, annoyed. It snarled when Spriditis threw a second one, but he quickly followed that pebble with a third. The bear lunged at him. Spriditis leaped into the barn and lay on the ground.

The beast followed him, which is exactly what Spriditis wanted. He jumped up and closed the door. The bear was now his prisoner!

Satisfied, he returned to the squire and said, "The bear is locked in the hay barn!"

"How did you do it?" asked the squire, impressed.

"None of your business!" answered Spriditis. "But if you must know, I grabbed him by the ears and dragged him into the barn. Don't believe me? Go look for yourself!"

At this point, the squire owed him his daughter's hand in marriage, but he wanted to put Spriditis to the test. "I'm impressed, but my daughter will not be. She has many suitors who could take down a bear. If you want to set yourself apart, you should take down the twelve bandits in the forest!"

Spriditis refilled his pockets with pebbles, went to the woods, climbed to the top of a tree, and waited. At midnight, the bandits showed up, sat down, and began eating and drinking. Once they finished, the ringleader ordered his assistant to check him for head lice. Spriditis threw a pebble at his head.

"Ouch!" said the bandit.

Spriditis threw a second one, followed by a third. With that, the bandit grabbed his assistant and began hitting him mercilessly.

"Help me!" yelled the poor assistant. All the other bandits began to fight, eventually falling to the ground breathless and bruised.

Spriditis climbed down the tree and ran back to the squire.

"The bandits are unconscious!" he announced.

"How did you do it?" asked the squire.

"That's none of your business!" answered Spriditis. "But if you must know, I knocked all twelve out with my fists. Don't believe me? Go look for yourself!"

Since Spriditis had passed even this test, the squire really should have kept his promise. Instead, he said, "Last night, one of my daughter's suitors managed to take down thirteen bandits. If you really want to impress her, you should get rid of the army that has invaded the country!"

Spriditis asked him for white clothes and a white horse, and took off alone against the foreign army.

When his enemies saw him galloping up to them with his fluttering white tunic and his snow-white steed, they thought he was a magic spirit. Fearing for their lives, they fled. Finally, Spriditis could marry the squire's daughter, and they lived happily ever after.

The Princess and the Pea

"Remember: You're a prince and you will only marry a true princess!" the queen told the prince as he departed in search of a young woman to marry.

He met many nobles along the way, but none of them had the look and character of a true princess. Some were too haughty and wouldn't have been able to love their people, while others were too foolish and would have spent all their time organizing parties and balls. Finally, after many months of being let down, the prince returned home.

That night, a heavy storm broke out, the likes of which had never been seen before! There was a knock on the door, and when the butler opened it, he found a girl drenched from head to toe, wearing stained clothing and mud-covered shoes. She asked the royal family to let her stay the night, saying she was a princess and that her carriage had fallen into the river.

"We'll see about that!" thought the queen. She crept into the guest room and put a pea on the bed where the girl was to sleep, piling twenty mattresses and twenty comforters on top of it.

Meanwhile, the young prince had seen the girl and was captivated by her beauty, by the way she spoke, by her gentle, elegant manners, and by her sincere eyes. He didn't care if she was really a princess—all he wanted was to marry her. But the queen said he had to wait until morning to declare his love for her.

That night, the exhausted young woman tried to sleep. No matter what she did she couldn't find a comfortable position. Something in the bed was bothering her! The next day at breakfast, the queen asked if she had slept well.

"Not at all, Your Majesty. I'm sorry to say but there was something between the covers the bruised me!"

The queen realized that the girl was a true princess, with skin so delicate that she could feel a pea under twenty mattresses and twenty comforters. She happily agreed to the marriage, and the pea that made it all possible was kept in a small box and carefully guarded by the prince as if it was the most precious gem in the world.

The Liar

In a land far, far away, there once lived a king with a beautiful daughter who always lied. When she came of age, the king decided that his daughter would marry the man who managed to outdo her and make him say, "That's a lie!"

The news quickly spread around the world, even reaching a small village where a widow lived with her only son. He was an incurable liar. One day, the young man told his mother, "I want to marry the princess! With your blessing, I'll leave in a few days."

She agreed, and he set off. After walking for days, he reached the king's palace. The guards stopped him, asking what he wanted.

The young man replied, "I want to ask for the princess's hand in marriage!"

The guards brought him before the king, who looked at him, perplexed. He certainly didn't look like a nobleman! So, to challenge him and have a little fun, the king took him to a large meadow where his flocks and herds were grazing.

"Look at my livestock, young man, and tell me what you think!" said the king.

The young man, who was very clever, immediately realized how to trick the king. He said, "What do I think, Your Majesty? They're nothing special. You should see my mother's cattle! Just imagine: They're so big that a wedding banquet was once held under one's belly after a terrible storm had broken out. It saved the party!"

The king looked at him, doubtful and a little annoyed. He then took the young man to a beautiful vegetable garden where some beans stalks grew.

"Now, tell me, what do you think of my bean stalks?"

"Your Majesty, I'm sorry, but they aren't special at all. You should see my mother's garden!" said the young man.

The king was really mad now. He asked, "What's so special about your mother's bean stalks?"

"Well," replied the young man, "they're so tall that the tip of the shortest one reaches the clouds. One day, I went out into the garden to harvest some. I climbed up from leaf to leaf, grabbing the pods and throwing them in a bag. Once it was full, I threw it to the ground and kept climbing.

"At the top, I found a house with a flea resting on one the wall. Since I needed a bag, I killed the flea and put some of the beans I had gathered into its skin. By the time I started to climb back down, the leaves had dried up, and they broke under my feet. I ended up in a ravine, stuck between two rocks. I grabbed my knife, cut off my head, and sent it home to tell my family what had happened.

"Along the way, I met a fox who grabbed my head and ran off with it. I was really worried by then! I managed to free my body from the rocks and ran after the fox. When I caught up with him, I cut off a piece of his tail. Imagine my surprise, Your Majesty, when I saw that, on his tail, it was written that your father had been my father's servant!"

At that point, the king became enraged and yelled, "That's a lie!"

"Of course it is, Your Majesty, but it was you yourself who invited me to say it. Now, keep your word and let me marry your daughter," replied the young liar, satisfied.

And so it was. The princess and the young liar fell deeply in love and the wedding party was so great that it lasted a whole year.

The Boy Who Went to the North Wind

In a small town there lived a poor woman with only one son. One day, she asked the boy to fetch some flour from the pantry. As he was bringing it to his mother, the north wind arrived and carried it away. He went back to the pantry and got more flour, but once again the north wind took it from him. He tried a third time, but had no luck. The boy was so angry that he decided to find the north wind and make it give the flour back.

He started walking and finally reached the north wind, who asked him what he wanted.

"Obviously," said the boy, "I want you to give me my flour back. My family is poor and we can't afford to lose the little that we have!"

The wind replied, "I don't have your flour, but I will give you a magic tablecloth that will give you everything you desire. You just have to say: 'Tablecloth, spread out and set the table with the most delicious food there is!'"

The happy boy set out for home. Because the journey was long, he stopped at an inn. When it was time to eat dinner, he took out the tablecloth and said, "Tablecloth, spread out and set the table with the most delicious food there is!"

In a snap, a sumptuous banquet appeared. All of the guests were impressed but the scene especially drew the attention of the inn's owner. He stole the tablecloth and replaced it with a look-alike while everyone slept.

The next morning, the boy took the fake tablecloth and left. When he got home, he told his mother what had happened and pulled out the tablecloth to show her what it could do. He pronounced the magic words, but nothing happened. Disappointed, the boy decided to go back to the north wind.

When he got there, he told the north wind, "I want the flour that you took. The tablecloth you gave me is worthless."

The north wind responded, "I don't have your flour, but I will give you a billygoat that makes gold coins. All you have to do is say: 'Make money!'"

The boy took the goat and set off, stopping at the same inn. Before ordering dinner, he wanted to test out the billygoat. He was happy to see that the north wind hadn't tricked him, but the owner of the inn saw the scene and swapped out the magical goat with a normal one as soon as the boy fell asleep.

Once he got home, the boy wanted to show his mother the goat's powers, but it didn't do as promised!

The boy returned to the north wind, who gave him a walking stick and said, "This walking stick isn't like the others. If you say, 'Stick, attack!' it will start hitting until it hears, 'Stick, stop!'"

The boy headed home. He stopped at the inn again, but by now he had realized what had happened to the tablecloth and the goat. After dinner, he lay down on a bench and pretended to sleep. The greedy innkeeper wanted the stick's magic powers, so he decided to steal it and replace it with another. When the innkeeper got close, the boy yelled, "Stick, attack!"

The stick began hitting the innkeeper, who cried out, "Please, tell it to stop. I'll give you the tablecloth and goat back!"

The boy stopped the stick.

With his belongings returned to him, the boy took the tablecloth, the goat, and the stick and set off on his journey home, where he finally showed his mother the power of the gifts he received from the north wind.

The Fox and the Stork

One day, a fox decided to invite a stork to dinner, but she didn't do much to prepare the meal. All she gave the stork was a pale, light broth served on a plate.

You can imagine how the stork felt! He definitely expected something nicer than broth, and perhaps better suited to a bird. With his long beak, the poor thing could barely get even a sip of the broth, which the fox finished in an instant.

Back home with an empty stomach, the stork decided that he would get revenge for the disrespect the fox had shown him.

After a few days, he went to the fox and invited her to lunch. The fox, who was a hearty eater, was happy to accept.

The stork got to work and prepared a succulent meat dish, cutting it into pieces and cooking it in a sauce that smelled wonderful. The fox couldn't wait to eat the delicious food!

Finally, the stork brought the meal and served it in a long, narrow-necked pot. The fox tried and tried, but she couldn't reach into the pot to get to the meat inside. The stork had no problem at all and ate his food without much effort.

This time, it was the fox who went home hungry, with an empty stomach and her tail between her legs. Perhaps she finally learned her lesson: Treat others as you wish to be treated.

The Spell of the Spring

In a town far, far away, a man lived with his three daughters. One sad day, he got sick and not even the most powerful wizards could cure him.

"If only I could drink the water from the magic spring!" cried the man.

His oldest daughter decided to get some water from the enchanted spring and bring it to him. After a long journey, she reached the spring, but when she was about to get the water, a voice said to her, "You can have the water only if you promise to marry me!"

The frightened girl ran home without the water.

The middle sister attempted to get the water as well, but as she was about to fill the jug, she too heard a voice say, "You can have the water only if you promise to marry me!"

Scared out of her wits, the girl returned home with an empty jug. It was then the youngest sister's turn. Katia set out on her journey. At the spring, she got close to the water and heard the same voice say, "You can have the water only if you promise to marry me!"

To save her father, she said yes, filled the jug with the water, and took it home. Her father drank it and immediately felt stronger.

One evening, a strange being covered in a wolf's pelt knocked at the door. Katia opened it, and the mysterious visitor reminded the frightened girl of her promise. Then he let the wolf pelt fall to the ground, revealing himself to be a handsome, strong young man. Astonished, Katia stared at him as he said, "I will visit you every night, but at midnight I must leave you. Because of a spell cast by the sorceress of the spring, I cannot show my face to anyone but you, as you agreed to marry me before you knew me. If anyone else discovers what I look like, I will be forced to disappear."

Katia promised she would keep his secret. The young man told her that his name was Stanislas. As promised, he returned to visit the maiden every night, but when he heard the last chime of midnight, he hid under the wolfskin and fled.

After some time, Katia needed to confide in someone and she told their secret to her father. Hoping to be able to break the spell, he stole the wolf hide and burned it. When the clock struck midnight and Stanislas couldn't find his cloak, he said, "Now we can no longer see each other. I must leave for a distant land beyond the sea. If one day you want to join me, you must wear iron shoes and fill an iron cauldron with your tears."

Katia began to cry. Soon she had shed enough tears to fill an entire iron cauldron. She decided to go look for him, so her father made her some iron shoes and she set off.

The journey was long and the metal shoes hurt her feet terribly. One evening, she met an old man who lived in a hut. He asked her, "Who are you and how did you manage to get here?"

Katia told him her story. The old man listened and said, "Let's ask the moon for news of your lost love."

The moon said she had never seen the young man, but advised the maiden to go to her brother, the sun, who reached even the most distant places with his rays.

Katia went to the sun, bringing a walnut the moon had given her. The sun had never met Stanislas, but he gave her another walnut and suggested that she speak to the wind. The wind listened to Katia's tale, then said, "Your beloved lives beyond the sea, but he is the prisoner of another woman. I'll take you to him."

He led the young woman to a town beyond the sea, where Stanislas was being hid prisoner by the witch of the spring. Before the wind left, he gave Katia a third walnut.

When she entered the town, Katia pretended to be a princess and asked if she could stay with the sorceress. The sorceress agreed and invited her to a party that evening. The young woman realized that the witch just wanted to see if she had a dress worthy of a princess. While she thought hard about what to do, she accidentally broke a walnut, and an incredible silver dress tumbled out.

When the witch saw the dress, she wanted it for herself and she said she was willing to offer Katia anything in return. Katia replied she would trade the dress for a day with Stanislas.

The witch accepted, but first made the young man drink a potion that took his memories. In vain, Katia tried to remind Stanislas about their life together, pointlessly talking to him about their love.

The next evening, Katia broke the second walnut, which held a dress the color of the sun. Once again, the witch asked to have it for herself, granting Katia's request to spend a day with Stanislas, and once again the witch gave him the memory-erasing potion.

The following night, a beautiful dress came out of the third walnut, as light as the wind. Katia gave it to the witch in exchange for a day with Stanislas, but this time, Katia had discovered the witch's cruel trick. Katia replaced the magic potion with water. Finally, Stanislas remembered the spring, the wolf hide, and their love story. He promised to never leave her side ever again.

Furious, the sorceress realized there was nothing she could do and disappeared forever.

The Little Mermaid

Once upon a time, in a kingdom far beneath the ocean, there lived half-human, half-fish creatures called mermaids. They were ruled over by the King of the Sea, who resided with his beautiful daughters in a wonderful palace decorated with shells and mother-of-pearls. The youngest mermaid was curious about the lives of humans, and she often swam up to the surface to spy on them.

One day, she saw a magnificent sailboat on the horizon. There was a party underway in honor of the prince, and the ship was adorned with hundreds of lanterns.

Suddenly the wind began to blow, the waves grew bigger, and the ship began to sink. The little mermaid dove down deep into the water to save the prince. She swam with all her might until she reached a beach, where she laid the unconscious young man on the sand. After hiding among the rocks, she began to sing a sweet song to wake him, watching over the prince until someone came help him.

The little mermaid returned to the sea, though she often visited that beach, hoping to see him again.

Seasons passed and the the mermaid's sadness was increasingly evident. The King of the Sea and his mother, who the young mermaid often confided in, were both very worried. After much hesitation, the little mermaid's grandmother decided to tell her about the sea witch.

"If you're only happy when you're on land, go see her. She'll help you, but . . . "

Without waiting one moment more, the little mermaid swam to the the sorceress's cave.

"I know what you wish for," sneered the witch, who offered her a deal. The witch would give her the appearance of a human girl in exchange for her wonderful voice.

The little mermaid drank the magic potion the witch gave her. A few seconds later, legs took the place of her tail, but when she tried to scream for joy, no sound came out of her mouth.

The swim from the depths of the sea was tiring, and she fell asleep as soon as she reached land. When she awoke, her eyes met those of the prince. Like her, he often came to the beach hoping to find the young woman with the beautiful voice who had saved him.

But the little mermaid couldn't talk, and couldn't explain that she was the one who had sung the song he heard. She fell into despair at seeing the prince so sad.

In the meantime, the King of the Sea was worried over his daughter's disappearance. He learned what the witch had done and, enraged, he went up to the surface, planning to bring the little mermaid home.

Instead, when he saw that his daughter was so in love, he took pity on her and decided to give her back her voice. She could once again sing like she had that fateful day on the rocks. The prince immediately recognized her and promised they would never be separated again.

The Steadfast Tin Soldier

One day, an old man who loved to make toys decided to create a small army of toy soldiers from an old tin ladle.

The boy who received them as a gift put them in a row on the table. They were all identical, except one, which had only one leg because there wasn't enough tin to complete it. The boy immediately became fond of it and the one-legged soldier became his favorite toy.

The table also held a wonderful cardboard castle with windows that revealed a balllroom inside. A young girl with perfect features stood in the castle's front door. She was made of cardboard like the castle, and wore a fine gauze dress and extended her arms above her head. She was a ballerina, and she stood balanced on one toe, with her other leg bent back and partially hidden beneath her skirt. The toy soldier thought that she, like him, had only one leg and was enchanted by her. Determined to meet her, he hid behind a cookie tin so he wouldn't be put back in his box. When evening fell and the family went to sleep, the toys held a party. They all laughed and played. Only two figures remained motionless: the ballerina and the tin soldier. He couldn't take his eyes off her, but he couldn't work up the courage to talk to her.

At midnight, the soldier finally tried to speak to the ballerina. Just as he reached her, there was a sharp click and the lid of the cookie tin opened. Out came a little devil, who also was in love with the ballerina. In a jealous rage, he yelled at the soldier, "No one can take my place next to the pretty ballerina!"

The next morning, the boy noticed that the tin soldier was outside of the box, so he placed him on the windowsill. A gust of wind blew the window open. The soldier fell out, ending up wedged in the cobblestones below. The boy ran into the street to look for him, but couldn't find him. In the meantime, a thunderstorm broke out, flooding the street.

When the rain stopped, two children saw the tin soldier and decided to sail him down the stream of water formed by the storm. They built a paper boat and put the soldier in it. As soon as they put it on the water, the fragile boat was sucked up by the current and sucked into a gutter.

The toy soldier's adventure seemed to go on forever, until he thought he saw a glimmer of light. The small stream emptied out, via a waterfall, into a big canal! The boat plunged and the soldier fell into the water, where a big fish swallowed him up.

As fate would have it, the fish soon ended up in a fisherman's net and was taken to the market. The fish was purchased by the cook who worked for the parents of the child who had received the tin soldier as a present. The soldier was found in the fish's belly and given back to the child, who put him on the table. The soldier was happy. He looked lovingly at the ballerina, who returned the look with the same tenderness.

Suddenly, one of the younger children grabbed him and threw him into the fireplace. Now all hope was lost! They were separated once again.

Then, the front door swung open and a gust of wind blew the castle and the ballerina straight into the fireplace. The cardboard instantly caught fire.

The next day, the fireplace was cleaned and the ashes were collected with a shovel. The two star-crossed lovers managed to find each other once again.

The Brave Chicken

Once upon a time, there was an old peasant who was so poor that he often didn't have enough to eat. He only had one rooster, which he saw as a burden. He complained about it all the time, saying sorrowfully, "If he at least was a hen, I could have fresh eggs every day. But a rooster is useless!"

The rooster was a bit disheartened, so one day he set out to the village to prove how useful he could be. Along the way, he saw a sack, which he picked up with his beak. Imagine his surprise when he saw the sack was full of golden coins!

He turned to go home right away, hoping to bring the loot to his owner. On his way back, he was attacked by two bandits, who stole the golden coins and threw the rooster down a well. The rooster refused to be defeated! He drank all the water, crawled out of the well, and chased after the thieves. When he reached them, they captured him again and threw him into a fireplace.

Refusing to give up, the rooster spat all the water he drank onto the fire and saved himself. When he caught up with the bandits again, they tied him up and locked him in the cave they were using to hide their stolen treasure. Once he was alone, the brave animal freed himself, swallowed all the coins that he could, and ran back home, where his owner welcomed him with a big party. From that day on, the peasant saw the brave rooster as his friend and most precious possession.

Bamboo and the Queen Bee

Once upon a time, there was a couple that longed for a child but couldn't have one. One day, the husband went to the forest to cut some bamboo. As the man was about to begin his task, he heard a tiny voice begging him not to harm it. Shocked, he asked, "Where are you?"

The voice answered, "In this piece of bamboo!"

What a surprise it was to look down and see a tiny baby with the face of a frog. The man and his wife decided to keep the baby and name him Bamboo.

As the years passed, the child grew into a kind boy who tried to help his father in any way he could. On his eighteenth birthday, his parents gave him a nice suit and a sword. They sent him to the market to sell the rice they had grown and to buy some fabric. Bamboo set out, crossing through the forest. There he met a hungry lion.

Bamboo told him, "I don't have anything for you. Come back tomorrow!"

The lion, responded, "You're wrong. I see something I can eat. You!"

So Bamboo took a decisive step forward and said, "Get out of here, unless you want to meet my sword!"

The lion, frightened, ran off with his tail between his legs!

The young man was almost through the forest when he came across a bee, who asked him to help his queen.

The queen was a tiny, beautiful young woman with two delicate silver wings. She had been flying amid the flowers when she was caught in a spider's web. Bamboo freed her, and the bee queen gave him three melon seeds in thanks, saying, "These seeds will make your greatest wishes come true, if you want them to!"

Bamboo took them and continued on his way. He went to the market, completed all of the errands his parents had entrusted him with, and began heading home. In the forest, he once again ran into the lion, who was even hungrier. Bamboo thought of scaring him off, and suddenly the lion fled in terror. Bamboo was confused until he realized that he had one less seed in his pocket. They really were magic!

He then wished to be a handsome young man and to see the marvelous queen of the bees again. Two seeds disappeared. Bamboo became a handsome young man and the bee queen appeared, but she had grown to the size of a human.

The pair was soon married and they lived happily ever after.

The Wind and the Sun

One day, the wind and the sun began fighting. The wind loudly proclaimed that he was the strongest, and the sun, in turn, said he was the greatest force on Earth. Unable to reach an agreement, they decided to put themselves to the test.

They saw a traveler who was walking along a trail, and decided that whoever managed to remove his clothes would be declared the strongest.

Without hesitating, the wind began to blow but that just made the man wrap himself up in his cloak.

Unwilling to give up, the wind began blowing harder, but the traveler just bowed his head and tightened his scarf around his neck. Disappointed, the wind had to admit he had failed.

Now it was the sun's turn. After clearing the sky of clouds, he began to shine. The man suddenly felt quite hot, so he removed his cloak.

The sun kept shining, increasing the heat of his rays.

Red from the heat, the man looked at the river he'd been traveling along. Without a second thought, he undressed and jumped into the cool water below.

The sun smiled up in the sky, while the defeated wind ran to hide in a faraway place.

The Fox and the Brahmin

There once was a Brahmin, a kind of Indian priest, who was very good and charitable, but also very naive.

One day, as he traveled to preach in a village beyond the woods, he come across a tiger locked in a cage. The Brahmin felt bad for the tiger and wanted to free it even though he knew tigers were man-eaters!

The beast promised the Brahmin that he wouldn't hurt anyone, so the good man opened the cage.

The tiger was barely out of the cage when he turned on the man. "You fool! Did you really think I wouldn't eat you, as hungry as I am?" he said.

The Brahmin replied, "Before you eat me, let's ask this tree what it thinks you should do."

The tree said, "Men certainly haven't been kind to me. I offer them shelter from the rain and cool shade on hot days. In exchange, they cut my branches, they cut my roots, and they've cut down my friends. As far as I'm concerned, you can eat him!"

The Brahmin saw a donkey in the clearing and asked him the same question, but the donkey answered, "Men are wicked! They exploit us all our lives and when we're old and weak, they abandon us. So, go ahead! Eat him!"

At that very instant, a fox showed up and the Brahmin said to the tiger, "Let's ask him what he thinks. If he says to eat me, I won't object!"

The fox looked at the tiger and said, "Are you making fun of me? How could such a big tiger fit in such a small cage?"

A bit annoyed, the tiger said it was possible. But the fox insisted. "Come on! I don't believe it!"

Angrily, the tiger got back into the cage and the fox quickly closed the iron gate. Then he said to the Brahmin, "In life, it isn't enough to be good and generous. You have to be a little cunning, too!"

The Brahmin then decided to go home and meditate about what had happened that day and what he had learned from the fox.

How to Get Rich

Once there was a peasant who decided to travel the world in search of a fortune. The day he set off, he spotted five golden coins on the road. He happily picked them up and continued, whistling as he went. When he reached the next town, he headed into an inn to get something to eat. He tried to order, but the owner looked at him and said, "Why should I serve you? I doubt you have the money to pay me!"

The peasant smiled and put a coin on the table. "Keep the rest for your trouble," he said.

The innkeeper then thought that the peasant was the king's son dressed as a beggar. When the peasant finished his drink, he called the innkeeper over and asked who the richest man in the city was. The man replied, "The owner of the baths!"

"Great," said the peasant. "I'll go to the public baths. At noon on the dot would you please bring me a cup of coffee and a pipe? Then tell the barber to come give me a shave and a haircut, and tell the cook to bring me a delicious lunch."

The owner of the baths was standing at the building's entryway. When he saw the peasant, he said, "These baths are for the rich. The poor go to the river!"

The peasant smiled and sat down on the steps. The janitor of the baths arrived and rudely told him to leave, as it wasn't a place for beggars. At that moment, precisely at noon, the innkeeper walked up with a tray bearing a coffee and a pipe. The barber was behind him and the chef followed with an extravagant lunch. They all bowed once they reached the peasant.

The janitor looked at them suspiciously until they told him that the beggar was actually the king's son in disguise. Once he heard that, the man invited the peasant to come in and ran to his boss to tell him who their special guest was. The owner of the baths began to worry. "I'll end up in prison! The king will have my head!" he said.

He ran home and filled a sack with gold coins to bring to the peasant, who had bathed, eaten, and shaved, and was sipping his coffee as he puffed on his pipe. With a smile, the peasant told the owner that he would accept his gift as an apology. Then he set out back home.

When the peasant reached the place where he had found the coins that morning, he grabbed five coins from his sack and placed them on the ground. Everyone in the village was astonished at his sudden wealth.

The peasant said, "It's easy. Leave the village in the morning and, along the way, you'll find five golden coins. By the time evening falls, you'll have a sack full of them!"

The next day, every peasant in the village headed out on that same road. Strangely, no one found a single coin and they all were just as poor as ever.

Ricky of the Tuft

Once upon a time, there was a king and a queen who wanted a child more than anything else in the world. Finally their child was born, but he was truly ugly. He had a silly tuft of hair that stood straight up on his head, which earned him the nickname Ricky of the Tuft. At his baptism, a fairy gave the boy a special gift: The child would be intelligent, and also have the power to make whoever he loved equally as wise.

Meanwhile, the queen of a nearby land gave birth to two girls. One of them was beautiful, while the other was ugly. They called for the fairy who was at Ricky's baptism and asked her to use her powers on the two princesses.

"Don't despair," said the fairy. "While your younger daughter will never be beautiful, she will be so smart that none who meet her will even consider her looks. Your older daughter, on the other hand, will grow to be beautiful, but also quite stupid. However, she will make the person she loves beautiful as well."

Years passed and the younger twin got uglier while the older one became ever more beautiful. Yet, while everyone was drawn to the prettier sister at first, soon they grew tired of her and gathered around the smarter one to enjoy her company.

The pretty young maiden suffered terribly because of it, so one day she ran off to cry in the park, where she met an ugly man. It was Ricky of the Tuft, who had fallen in love with her when he saw her portrait. He had traveled for days to meet her.

When the prince saw her tears, he asked, "How could a girl as beautiful as you be so sad?"

"I'd rather be ugly and smart! Like my sister!" responded the princess.

"When I was born, I was gifted the ability to give the person that I choose the intelligence they desired. I love you and, if you promise to marry me, I will give you the very thing you dream of," said Ricky.

"I understand why you hesitate. I know how I look," he continued. "Here's what we'll do. If you accept my proposal, you'll have a year to think it over, starting from today. In the meantime, I'll give you the intelligence you desire."

The princess accepted. She felt a change come over her and, from that moment on, proved to be quite intelligent.

Young suitors from nearby kingdoms competed for her hand, but the princess rejected them all.

After a year, the king asked her to choose her groom. The princess told him that she needed to think, then headed out to the park. As she walked, she saw various servants running to and fro with plates, torches, and beautiful tablecloths.

She followed them and saw that they were setting up an incredible feast. Surprised, she asked what they were celebrating. They said they were setting up the wedding banquet for Ricky of the Tuft.

Only then did the princess remember that one year ago she had promised to marry Ricky, who walked up to her at that very moment.

"I hope you are here to keep your word," said the prince.

"To be honest, I still haven't decided. I'm afraid my answer will disappoint you."

"Tell me, aside from my looks, what is it you don't like about me?" asked Ricky.

"Nothing. You're smart, interesting. . ."

"Well, then, I am happy. Because the fairy that gave me the gift of bestowing intelligence on my beloved gave you the gift of bestowing beauty on yours. You have the power to make me the most handsome of men. You just have to love me enough to will it so," replied Ricky.

"In that case, I wish with all my heart for you to become my groom!"

As soon as she said those magic words, Ricky of the Tuft turned into the most handsome man on Earth. They were married the very next day and lived happily ever after.

Tam Lin

Once upon a time, a nobleman had a daughter named Janet. One day, the adventurous young girl decided to explore the woods near her house. She soon came to a clearing filled with beautiful wild roses. Janet decided to pick some for her mother and sisters, but as soon as she grabbed one, a young knight sprung from the earth. "How dare you pick these roses!" he said.

"I just wanted to give my mother and my sisters a small gift," Janet said.

The knight looked at her for a long time and said, "I'm supposed to protect this forest, but I would give you just about anything you want! My name is Tam Lin."

On hearing his name, Janet realized he was an elf and was a bit frightened, but Tam Lin reassured her. "Don't fear. I'm human, like you. I was kidnapped by the Queen of the Elves years ago and, since then, my job has been to guard the forest during the day. At night, I return to their kingdom, where the queen holds me prisoner. All I want is to break the spell!'"

When Janet offered to help him, Tam Lin said, "Tonight is Halloween, and the elves will travel here to hunt. Go to the crossroads at the forest's entrance. When you see me pass by, grab on to me and don't let go, no matter what happens!"

Janet went to the crossroads that night and waited for the elves to ride past. When she saw Tam Lin appear, she jumped to grab him, holding him close. Suddenly the young man became a small lizard, then a scary snake, and then a red-hot iron rod. But Janet wasn't scared and didn't give in to the pain. The Queen of the Elves soon realized she had lost, and let Tam Lin go.

Janet and Tam Lin were married and lived happily ever after.

The Princess in the Tower

Once upon a time, a king and queen lived happily with their only daughter. One terrible day, the queen fell ill and died.

After a few years, the king decided to remarry, choosing a noble widow with two daughters as his bride. But, as often happens in fairy tales, the new queen was a powerful witch. When the king departed on a long journey, the wicked stepmother locked the princess and her servants in a tall tower in the thick of the forest. All were turned into mice, except the princess's lady-in-waiting, who was turned into a crow.

Satisfied, the witch left with a cackle, believing that she would never hear from the young girl again.

In a kingdom not far away, a king lived with his three sons. The king was now old and wanted the young men to get married. One day, he summoned them, handed them each a golden apple, and said," Throw these apples in different directions and follow where they lead. At the end of your journey, you will find your future bride."

The two older brothers threw their apples and followed them to the neighboring kingdom, where they met the witch's daughters and fell in love. The younger brother did the same, but his apple began rolling toward the forest. He followed it to a clearing, where a crow grabbed his attention and led him to a tower hidden among the trees. He entered the tower and was surprised to find lots of friendly mice, who warmly welcomed him. In their midst stood a beautiful mouse. She did her best to make the prince's life pleasant, and they became fast friends.

One day the mouse said, "Why don't we get married? We have so much fun together and, even though I'm a mouse, you could learn to love me."

The prince agreed. After all, his feelings for her were quite magical.

The young man took all of the mice and began the journey home to present his future bride to his father. However, as they came closer to the castle, he began to question his decision. When he saw the magnificent parade that followed his brothers and their beautiful brides, he truly began to fret.

By the time he stood before his father, he was filled with doubt. But suddenly, the mice began turning back into humans, and his beloved turned into one of the most beautiful princesses he had ever seen. His love had gotten the better of the cruel spell! The two were married a few days later and lived happily ever after.

The evil stepmother was exiled while the stepsisters, who hadn't known of their mother's wicked plan, married the other two princes.

The Snowy Mountains and the Bird of Happiness

A long time ago, Tibet had become a dark, dark place. The sun never shone and there were no plants and almost no water. Many people blamed this on the bird of happiness, who had flown away and hidden in the land of eternal snow where it had been captured by three ferocious dragons.

One day, a brave young man named Ming decided to free it. He set out on foot but soon found his path blocked by a fire-breathing dragon. "Where do you think you're going?" the dragon said.

Ming told the dragon he was going to free the bird of happiness. The dragon replied, "My brothers and I will never let you!" He slapped his tail on the ground, and an impenetrable thicket of brambles appeared.

Ming wasn't scared and paid no mind to the wounds inflicted by the thorns as he walked through the thicket. Soon, he found himself standing before a dragon more fearsome than the first. "You'll never complete your mission!" the dragon said.

The dragon slapped his tail on the ground and created a vast desert, but not even that could stop Ming. He overcame this test as well despite his thirst and hunger.

A third dragon waited for him at the border of the desert. When Ming reached the dragon, it struck out, blinding him. Ming wandered aimlessly until he came near the place where the bird of happiness was being held captive.

The bird called out to him as he approached. When Ming reached the bird, it touched his eyes, restoring his sight and healing his wounds. Ming freed the miraculous creature, who took flight and brought him back to Tibet. From that day on, the country was happy and flourished once again.

Thumbelina

Once upon a time there was a woman who really wanted a daughter. She went to an old fairy for help. The fairy gave her a barley seed and told her to plant it. After a little while, a wonderful flower sprouted from the earth, holding a tiny, beautiful girl. The woman called her Thumbelina, because the girl was no bigger than her thumb. She used a walnut shell as a cradle, made a mattress out of violet leaves and gave Thumbelina a rose petal as a blanket.

One dark night, a big, slimy toad saw Thumbelina sleeping in her cradle on the windowsill and decided she would be the perfect wife for his son. He kidnapped her and carried her to the pond at the back of the garden, setting her down on a large water lily so she couldn't escape.

When she woke up, poor Thumbelina looked around and saw only dark water! Frightened, she began to cry, drawing the attention of the fish in the pond. They decided to help her, pushing the water lily ashore.

Thumbelina thanked the fish and started walking across the wheat field that extended out from the forest, seeking help. She reached the house of a country mouse, who offered to host her for the winter.

One day, the mouse's old friend, Mr. Mole, came to visit. He lived in a large burrow nearby and had a big pantry full of food. Mr. Mole told them that he had dug a tunnel from his house to theirs, and invited them to visit. They came across a wounded bird—a swallow—on the path to Mr. Mole's house and Thumbelina felt very sorry for her.

That night, Thumbelina ventured out into the tunnel, bringing some hay to cover her. She took care of the poor bird the entire winter, nursing the wound that had prevented her from flying to warmer places with her flock.

When spring came, the swallow was completely healed and ready to fly away. She offered Thumbelina a ride on her back so that the girl could leave with her, but Thumbelina was grateful to the mouse, and didn't want to leave her alone.

When autumn came, Thumbelina grew sad. Soon it would be the cold, dark, boring winter, and she'd only have the mouse and Mr. Mole for company. One afternoon, she heard the unmistakable cry of the swallow, who once again asked her if she wanted to leave. This time, Thumbelina accepted her offer. She sat on the bird's back and the two flew to the lake where the swallow had built her nest. She set Thumbelina down on a lily and said goodbye.

When the girl turned to get her bearings, she was surprised to find a tiny boy, just her size, on the flower beside her. He was the king of the lilies. He had a shiny crown and two beautiful mother-of-pearl wings. The two fell in love and decided to marry.

The day of their wedding, Thumbelina received two beautiful wings of her own so she could fly from one flower to the next. After the wedding, the swallow said goodbye to the new queen and flew off to distant shores, telling the wonderful story of Thumbelina wherever she went.

The Wolf and the Fox

There was once a wolf who enjoyed bossing around a fox. The fox begrudgingly obeyed, as the wolf was the stronger of the two.

One day, the wolf said, "Fox, get me something to eat, or I'll eat you."

The fox replied, "I know a farm where there are two sheep. If you want, we can get one."

The wolf agreed, so the fox stole a sheep, brought it to the wolf, and went to bed. The wolf, however, still wasn't satisfied. He wanted the other sheep as well, so he went to get it. He was so noisy that he woke the farmers, who chased him into the woods.

When he reached the fox, panting and angry, he yelled, "You really tricked me! I wanted to get the other sheep, but the farmers made a fool out of me!"

The fox replied, "Well, why are you so greedy?"

The next day, at lunch, the wolf said, "Fox, get me something to eat, or I'll eat you."

The fox replied, "I smell fritters. Let's go get some."

When night fell, the fox crept around the farm, then snuck in through the kitchen window. She sniffed and sniffed until she found the plate with the fritters, which she brought to the wolf before continuing on her way.

When he had eaten them all, the wolf realized he wanted more. He went back to the farm, but he dropped the plate as he was leaving. It made such a ruckus that the farmer's wife came to investigate the noise and began throwing pots and pans at the wolf. Many of them hit their mark! The wolf ran back to the fox with a big bump on his head.

"Thanks to you and those fritters, I got hit three times with a pan!" he said.

The fox replied, "Well, why are you so greedy?"

The third day, the wolf said again, "Fox, get me something to eat, or I'll eat you."

The fox replied, "I know a butcher who keeps his meat in the cellar. Let's go get some."

"All right, but I'm going to go with you this time so I can get as much food as I want and you can help me escape."

The cellar was filled with lots and lots of meat, and the wolf jumped right in.

The fox ate happily too, but every so often she stopped to look out of the hole that they had entered through.

"Fox, why do you keep running back and forth?" asked the wolf with his mouth full.

"I'm making sure no one is coming," replied the clever fox.

When the butcher arrived, the fox quickly jumped out of the hole. The wolf tried to follow her, but he had eaten so much that he couldn't get through. He was trapped! The butcher easily caught him, and the fox ran into the woods, happy to never see that old glutton again.

Winter and Spring

One day, Winter, a surly, conceited old man, met Spring, a young lady. The old season said, "My dear, you don't know what it means to be decisive and determined. When your time comes, people and animals rush out of their homes or their dens and fill the fields that you have made bloom with so much care and effort. They tear up young shrubs, trample the grass, and soak up all the rays of the wonderful sun that grows hotter the moment you arrive. Your fruit is picked and eaten without restraint and then, with all the racket they make, they don't even let you rest peacefully. I, on the other hand, instill awe and reverent respect with my fog, cold, and ice. People stay home and go out as little as possible, leaving me be."

Young Spring replied, "But my arrival is desired by all and people love me. You can't imagine what it means to be so appreciated. It's a wonderful feeling that you'll never experience because the cold that you bring freezes even the warmest hearts."

Winter paused to reflect in silence. Perhaps being appreciated and loved by others was indeed a good feeling!

The Rooster, the Dog, and the Fox

One morning, a cunning rooster was perched on a branch to guard his henhouse. Along came a fox, who greeted him and said, "My friend, we're no longer at war. Peace has settled about the land. Come down. I'd like to give you a hug! Don't be afraid; you can trust me!"

With a big smile, she continued, "Hurry up though. I have to tell one hundred other animals, maybe even more. Now you're free to go where you want and we'll be the best of friends! We'll throw a big party with fireworks. We'll be happy and have fun! Come on, let me give you a kiss to prove it."

"My friend," replied the clever rooster, "your words are moving and I'm grateful. But I would like to make peace in a more suitable way, by also hugging the greyhound that's quickly running toward us. He's surely one of the messengers sent to spread the word. I'll happily get down once he gets here. That way we can have a group hug."

Alarmed, the fox looked at the road and said, "You greet him. I can't wait, I'm already short on time. Maybe tomorrow we can all celebrate properly."

She ran off to the countryside, disappointed that her carefully planned trick had failed. Seeing the fox run off with her tail between her legs, the old rooster smiled and recited a famous saying. It's twice as satisfying to trick he who wanted to trick you.

The Nymph and the Fisherman

Once upon a time, a fisherman lived a quiet life in a small hut by the sea. He spent his days fishing, then went to the market to sell what he managed to catch. It was a simple life that may seem boring to many, but he knew how to appreciate what he had and enjoy the beauty of nature all around him.

One morning, as he dropped his lure into the water, he smelled something so intensely sweet that it stunned him. He left his fishing rod and followed his nose. He reached the edge of the woods, where he found a beautiful veil that was giving off the scent. He decided to take it home and guard it like a treasure.

He climbed the tree and grabbed the veil. It was incredible, bright as the rays of the sun, sparkling like the stars in the sky, large but very light. The happy fisherman folded it and was about to head home when a young maiden arrived.

"Wait, that's mine! It's the veil of the celestial nymphs. Give it back to me please," she said.

The fisherman, however, was not willing to part with his treasure. "If it's so valuable, I'd be a fool to give it back to you."

As he spoke, he looked up at the young woman. She was beautiful, with soft black hair that flowed down her shoulders and an incredible silver dress that lit up her face. He looked at her more closely and saw that she was crying.

"Please," she said with the sweetest voice he'd ever heard. "Give me back the veil so that I can return to my sisters."

The fisherman thought about it for a long time, and then answered, "I will give it back if you will stay here and dance for me."

"I'll do whatever you want! But give me back the veil!"

The fisherman hesitated, afraid that she would fly away as soon as she got the veil back. After a moment he agreed.

The young woman wrapped herself in the delicate veil and began to dance. No other mortal had ever seen a celestial nymph dance! The fisherman happily watched her twirl until the nymph slowly ascended toward the sky, disappearing into the fog.

He was briefly sad and lonely, but then peace came to his heart and the memory of the nymph comforted him. "What a wonderful day!" he thought. "I'm so lucky. As long as I live, I shall never forget that shining celestial nymph." Smiling, he returned to the sea and quietly resumed fishing.

Goldilocks and the Three Bears

Three bears lived in a house in the woods: Papa Bear, who was the biggest; Mama Bear, who was a little smaller; and Baby Bear, their cub. Everything in their house was made to fit them perfectly. Papa Bear had the biggest armchair, the largest cup, and the heaviest books. Mama Bear's were a bit smaller. The cub-sized things belonged to Baby Bear.

One day, the three of them decided to go for a walk in the woods to get some honey as they waited for their soup to cool. While they were gone, a very curious and slightly naughty girl named Goldilocks walked by their house.

Peeking into the window, she saw three bowls of steaming soup. Since she was quite hungry, she decided to go in and try them. She tried the largest bowl, but it was too hot. She tried the second, but it was too salty. She tried a spoonful of the soup in the smallest bowl, and it was so delicious that she ate it all.

She then sat in the biggest armchair, but it was too hard. The medium one was too soft, while the smallest one was just right. Too bad it broke as soon as she sat down!

Goldilocks went upstairs to look around, and found a bedroom with three beds. One was too tall, the one next to it was too narrow, and the smallest one was just her size. So, she lay down on it and soon fell fast asleep. Soon after, the bears came home to eat lunch.

"Who touched my soup?" asked Papa Bear, noticing his spoon was out of place.

"Someone's tasted mine!" said Mama Bear, pointing at some spilled soup.

"And who ate all of mine?" cried Baby Bear.

They saw Baby Bear's broken chair and decided to find the intruder. As soon as they got to the bedroom, Papa Bear noticed the messy covers on his bed, Mama Bear saw the rumpled up pillow, and Baby Bear found a girl asleep on his bed!

The bears gathered around her and yelled, "Who are you?"

Goldilocks awoke with a start and, seeing the angry bear faces, was so scared that she leaped out the window and escaped into the woods, swearing that she would never be so curious again!

The Town Mouse and the Country Mouse

One day, a country mouse was invited to lunch by his cousin, who lived in the city.

He was given a warm welcome and treated to a fine banquet, just for him, in the hopes that he would see the benefits of city life.

Comfortably seated around an exquisite carpet, the cousins chatted and ate various delicacies and food of all kinds. The town mouse told his guest of the wonders and opportunities of the city. The country mouse listened, fascinated. He was almost convinced that it might be time to leave his quiet home in the field, when they heard a terrible noise at the door.

The city mouse ran and hid, abandoning everything on the table, and his frightened cousin did the same.

When things quieted down again, the town mouse returned to his seat and tried in vain to convince his guest to follow suit. But his cousin was adamant: That was quite enough of city life for him!

"I wouldn't dream of staying here!" he declared. "Tomorrow you can come visit me in the countryside. We won't eat all this fancy food and the table setting won't be as refined, but no one will bother us at the top of a stalk of wheat. We'll be able to eat in peace. Without that, even a full belly isn't a pleasure!"

Cinderella

There was once a rich widower who decided to remarry so that he didn't have to leave his daughter alone when he went on long trips for his work as a merchant. He married a woman with two daughters, and was relieved that his daughter would have such good company. But after he departed, the stepsisters proved to be mean and spiteful, and their mother selfish and cruel. The stepmother forced the merchant's daughter to work in the kitchen and sleep among the cinders near the fireplace. Her clothes and hair soon turned the color of soot.

The two evil stepsisters, who never missed a chance to make fun of her, began calling her Cinderella. For years, Cinderella performed her humble tasks without asking for anything in return, but when the invitation to a royal ball arrived, she worked up the courage to ask her stepmother if she could go. The stepmother said no, taking her own daughters to the ball and leaving Cinderella alone for the night.

In tears, Cinderella hid in the garden until a small fairy appeared, determined to help her. The fairy first cast a spell and transformed a dishcloth into a beautiful dress, complete with two sparkling crystal slippers. Then she took a pumpkin from the garden

and turned it into a carriage with a touch of her wand. Four mice became beautiful white horses, and the dog was transformed into a fine coachman. Finally, Cinderella was ready for the ball. Before she left, the fairy warned her that the spell would be broken at midnight.

When Cinderella entered the ballroom, everyone turned to admire her and the prince asked her for a dance. As they danced, time seemed to stand still. But when the clock struck midnight, Cinderella remembered the fairy godmother's warning. She ran away, losing one of her crystal slippers in her haste.

The next day, the prince sent the grand duke to all the houses in the kingdom to have every young maiden try on the slipper, promising to marry whoever it fit. When they reached Cinderella's home, her stepsisters did everything they could to get their feet in the slipper, but in the end they had to give up.

As the grand duke turned to leave, he saw Cinderella in a corner and decided to give it one last try. To everyone's surprise, the slipper fit perfectly. She was immediately brought to the palace, where she married the prince in a wonderful wedding, and all her dreams came true.

The Fox and the Rooster

One day, a fox and a rooster were chatting when the fox asked, "How many tricks do you know?"

The rooster thought about it for a minute. He said, "I only know three. You?"

The fox smiled smugly. "My dear friend, I know seventy-three!"

"Wow, that's a lot! I don't believe it."

"If you don't believe me, put me to the test!" the fox said.

With that, the rooster asked his friend to show him one, just to get started.

The fox thought about it for a minute. "Well, my grandfather taught me how to close one eye and let out a loud cry," he said.

The rooster looked at him and exclaimed, "What kid of trick is that? Even I can do that!" He closed one eye and let out a high-pitched cry.

The eye he closed was the one closest to the fox, which is just what the fox wanted. He grabbed the rooster by the neck and started to run back to his den.

A woman in a nearby house witnessed the whole scene. When she saw the poor rooster being dragged away by the fox, she called out to him.

"You old trickster! Let that rooster go! He's mine!"

The rooster saw his chance and whispered to the fox, "Don't let her fool you. Tell her that I now belong to you."

The fox gladly took the rooster's advice and opened his mouth to speak, dropping the rooster. In a flash, the rooster flew to the roof of the house and, closing one eye, let out an impressive cry.

For once, it was the cunning fox who had been tricked by an equally clever rooster. The fox spent that night hungry and thinking about how foolish he had been!

The Hedgehog and the Hare

One day, a hedgehog and a hare met in the woods. After they had spoken for a while, the hare said, "You poor thing. With those short, crooked legs, it would take you an entire morning to walk half the distance I can cover in a minute."

Surprised, the hedgehog replied without thinking. "I can run just as well as you can. If we were to race each other, I surely would win!"

The hare couldn't help but laugh. "A race between a hedgehog and a hare? Sure, why not? Let's meet tomorrow. If you win, I'll tell everyone that you're the fastest animal in the forest. But if you lose, you have to admit you're the slowest."

At that point, the hedgehog had to accept the challenge. As he walked along the trail to his den, all he could think about was the mess he had gotten himself into.

When he got to his den, his wife noticed the worried look on his face and asked what had happened. The hedgehog told her that the hare had offended him and now he was in real trouble. His wife thought for a bit, and then lit up.

"I've got an idea. We'll teach that snobby hare a real lesson! Tomorrow, I'll hide near the finish line, while you meet the hare at the starting line. Once the race starts, you'll jump into a bush, while I'll leap out at the finish line. That way, that cocky hare will think you've beaten him!"

"What a great idea!" exclaimed the relieved hedgehog.

The next morning, Mr. Hedgehog met the hare to defend his honor, while his wife hid near the finish line. When the starting signal was given, the hare was off as fast as lightning. The hedgehog hid behind a bush after two short steps.

His wife jumped out near the finish line and said, "I won!"

Humiliated and exhausted, the hare didn't even noticed he had been tricked. Thanks to the clever hedgehogs, he stopped making fun of other animals and he never again boasted of being the fastest in the forest.

The Golden Oranges

The king's garden had trees from all over the world, but the rarest of them all was the one that grew golden oranges. The king guarded that precious tree jealously, even posting a soldier nearby day and night. One day, he found the sentry asleep. "How dare you sleep while carrying out your king's orders!"

"I'm sorry, Your Majesty. A goldfinch came and began singing such a sweet song that I couldn't help but fall asleep!"

The king decided that he would keep watch over the precious tree himself that night. The goldfinch returned. When the king heard the goldfinch's song, he too fell asleep and some of the golden oranges were stolen. Furious, the king issued a proclamation: Whoever captured that mouthy bird would be richly rewarded.

The next day, a young peasant showed up at court, carrying a cage with the goldfinch in it. "Here is the bird, Your Majesty. But I don't want gold and precious coins. As my reward, I desire the princess's hand in marriage."

The king, outraged, said that he would never let his only daughter marry a lowly peasant. Then he called for his guards to remove the man from the palace.

The King's tree was safe at last, but only because the imprisoned bird was so sad it didn't sing a single note. The princess couldn't stand the sight of that poor creature locked in a cage. She asked it, "Goldfinch, will you start singing again if I free you?"

The bird replied, "I can't sing as long as my owner is sadder than I am."

The princess, was shocked. "Your owner is that peasant?"

"Yes, Your Highness. But he isn't a peasant. He has a whole grove of golden orange trees and is richer than the king! From the moment he saw you, he has thought of nothing other than how to marry you!"

The princess was exited by that bit of news. She had been quite taken by the bird's owner, and she knew how greedy her father was.

The princess snuck the bird into her room and freed it. "Fly to your owner and tell him to return to court at once. Once my father finds out how rich he is, he'll surely approve of our marriage."

The princess knew her father well. As soon as he heard of the young man's incredible wealth, the king agreed to the wedding. The princess and the young man got married and lived happily ever after.

The Village of Sparrows

Young Tolau lived in a small village, working on his rice farm, which was the lushest in the land.

One evening, he saw an ominous dark cloud draw closer to his farm. He looked again and realized that it was actually a giant flock of sparrows. They reached his farm and destroyed his entire harvest before taking off to the east. All Tolau could do was wait for the next growing season and start again.

But the same thing happened the next year. The birds arrived and destroyed his entire harvest, leaving the neighboring farms untouched.

The following season, his rice grew tall and strong, and once again the sparrows came and destroyed it. At his wit's end, Tolau decided to set out and find the village of the sparrows.

He followed the flock east, keeping the birds overhead until he finally reached an eerily quiet village. The doors to all of the houses were open, but no one was around.

He walked to the prettiest house of them all, near a river. He peeked through the door and called out. When no one answered, Tolau went inside. The house had a single large room with a crystal floor and crystal ceiling. At the center of the room was a platform, with twenty silver steps that led to the top.

Tolau sat on the lowest step when a golden glass full of water and a golden bowl full of rice appeared before him. He didn't dare touch them!

Before long, an old woman appeared on the platform, asking him why he didn't eat the rice or drink the water.

Tolau replied that he wouldn't have dared, lest he be mistaken for a thief.

The woman invited him to eat and drink, which Tolau did happily. When he had his

fill, Tolau asked why the village was so empty and where all the rice came from, since he hadn't seen any rice paddies nearby.

The woman took him to a hill, where Tolau suddenly saw the same gray cloud that had turned his entire life upside down. The woman clapped her hands and numerous baskets appeared on the banks of the river. The sparrows dropped rice into them, then dove into the water.

As soon as they touched it, the birds turned into people. They gathered the baskets and headed to the village. The last of the group was a girl with very long black hair, who enchanted Tolau with her beauty.

"So, now you know why there are no rice paddies here," the old woman said. "Rice grows in many places. All we do is harvest it. A lot of that rice came from your land."

"Isn't that stealing?" Tolau asked.

"Yes, that's true, but the people of my village were once punished by being turned into sparrows, forcing us to steal rice to feed ourselves. Now the spell is broken, and we can go back to living like other people, growing rice and vegetables on our own land.

"The truth is, Tolau, that three seasons ago the punishment could have ended. But knowing that you were looking for a wife, I asked my people to keep turning into sparrows and stealing your rice so that you would end up here."

As the woman spoke, the young lady who had struck Tolau with her beauty approached them.

The woman continued, "I wanted my daughter to marry the most honest man in the world, and I can't think of anyone more honest than you."

The two were married a few days later and lived happily ever after.

The Snow Queen

Gerda and Kai were two inseparable friends. They lived next door to one another and spent their days playing in a garden amid the rose bushes. Every evening, when the sun began to set, Kai's grandmother would tell them their favorite fairy tale: The story of the cruel Snow Queen, an evil woman who would freeze lakes and rivers with her glare and turn the hearts of men to ice.

One winter evening, while his grandmother was telling the tale, a cold wind blew a window open. A snowflake got into Kai's eye and made its way to his heart, turning it to ice.

Kai became mean and selfish. His favorite game was tying his sled to carriages so that they would pull him down the road. It was very dangerous, but Kai had so much fun that he didn't care.

One day, he hooked his sled up to a particularly elegant carriage, which dragged him out of the town. When the carriage stopped, a woman stepped out. She was wrapped in a fur coat, and had skin white as snow and hair blue as ice. It was the Snow Queen!

She walked over to Kai and gave him a kiss that stole his memories. The Snow Queen brought Kai to her ice castle. When the boy didn't come home that night, everyone assumed he had been in an accident, but Gerda never stopped hoping that he would return.

Years passed, and Gerda eventually decided to look for her friend. The girl walked for days until she reached a small house where an old, lonely fairy lived. With a spell, the fairy erased Gerda's memory and convinced her to live with it.

A whole winter passed. When spring came, the rose bushes began to bloom and Gerda remembered the days she had spent playing in a garden with Kai. She wanted nothing more than to continue on her quest to find her long-lost friend. Seeing her so sad, the fairy let her depart and told her where to find the Snow Queen's palace.

Gerda entered the castle while the Snow Queen slept. Her breath froze in the cold air, but her heart warmed when she saw Kai. He was seated on a throne in the large hall, staring into space.

Gerda ran to hug him, crying tears of joy. One of her tears fell into Kai's eye and kept going until it reached his icy heart. It thawed him from the inside out, returning his memories along with his affection for Gerda.

The two friends escaped the Snow Queen's castle just as she awoke. The journey home was long, but they were so happy to see each other that they didn't even notice.

The Snake Prince

Once upon a time, there was a king and a vizier who were lifelong friends. When both of their wives were pregnant, the two decided that if one was a boy and one was a girl, the children would one day marry each other.

But while the king's child was a boy, he was born with the body of a snake! The vizier, on the other hand, had a beautiful baby girl with golden hair and emerald green eyes. They named her Esmeralda. The girl and the snake grew up together and became close friends.

One day, while they were playing, the snake shed his skin to reveal a handsome boy with fair skin and eyes as blue as the sea. Unfortunately, the young man soon donned his snake skin and returned to his previous form.

The king had witnessed the entire scene, hiding in secret. He asked Esmeralda to make sure that the next time, his son didn't turn back into a snake. When the prince next took on his human appearance, the girl burned the snake's skin. The young man looked at her in despair and vanished into thin air, leaving her in tears. The girl grew sad and lonely.

One day while walking along her usual path, the girl met an old witch, who said, "Your true love is very far away. You will wear out seven pairs of shoes before you find him!"

Esmeralda set off to search for him. She crossed dangerous forests and desolate lands, swam in the deepest waters of the sea and through tumultuous river rapids.

Finally, on the day she had worn out her seventh pair of shoes, she reached a castle perched on the side of a steep mountain. An old lion stood guard and asked her for something to eat. She offered him her last piece of dried meat. She then came across a line of ants, who asked her to help them rebuild their anthill. Esmeralda did this with great care. Once she reached the large castle door, she noticed it was a bit squeaky and used her last drop of oil to grease it. She finally walked into the castle, where an evil genie, jealous of the young prince's looks, had locked him in chains.

Esmeralda found her prince, hungry and cold, and freed him. The two tried to escape, but the genie yelled to the door, "Don't let them out!"

The door replied, "The princess greased my hinges and cared for me, so I'm going to let them go!"

Then the genie said to the ants, "Sting them and make sure they don't escape!"

"We will do no such thing!" the ants said. "She helped us and we're forever grateful!"

Finally, the genie turned to the lion and yelled, "Tear them to pieces! Both of them!"

"I will not!" answered the old beast. "She fed me and I won't betray her!"

Angrier than ever before, but unable to leave the castle, the genie disappeared in a puff of smoke.

Esmeralda and the prince made their way home, where they were married and lived a long, happy life together.

The Mouse and the Frog

One day, a handsome country mouse met a funny, rather ungraceful frog. The two became fast friends.

Some time later the frog asked the mouse how he got his food.

The mouse replied, "Actually, I'm not very good at that. I always have a hard time finding something to eat."

The frog thought about it for a minute, then answered, "What if I looked for food with you? If we work together, surely we'll find enough to eat. We could link ourselves with a chain; that way we won't get separated!"

The mouse thought it was a great idea and agreed. They tied themselves together with a chain and went out in search of food. They found some easily.

At the end of the day, they headed home full and happy. They were still chained together when they reached the pond where the frog lived. Without thinking, the frog dove into the water, dragging the poor mouse with him. The mouse began to scream and struggled not to drown.

A large bird heard the ruckus and, seeing the mouse with little strength left, thought he had found an easy dinner. Just as the mouse fell unconscious, the bird swooped down to the pond and grabbed him. The frog was pulled into the air along with him and began to scream as loudly as he could.

The frog's cries woke the mouse, who began to bite the bird's legs with his sharp little teeth. Surprised by the pain, the bird let go, dropping the mouse and the frog to the ground. Luckily, they landed without getting hurt! They quickly decided to free themselves from the silly chain that had caused them so much trouble.

The Panther

There was once a widow who lived in a small town with her son and two daughters. One day, the widow left her daughters in charge of the house while she took her baby boy to run some errands and visit her mother. Not long after she left, the poor woman was attacked by a panther. The panther stole her clothes, put them on, and knocked on the door of the widow's house.

"Open up kids, it's mom!" the panther said, trying to imitate the woman's voice.

The two girls looked outside suspiciously and said, "But our mother's hands aren't all black!"

Quickly, the panther replied, "Oh, I fell into a pile of soot!"

The young girls insisted, "Our mother's voice isn't so hoarse!"

"I know—I caught a cold!" said the panther.

"But mom, even your face looks different!" they replied.

"I worked in the garden all day yesterday and I got a sunburn."

By now, the girls had realized that there was a ferocious panther at their door and not their sweet mother. They were quite scared!

Their turtle, who had watched the whole scene without making a peep, finally spoke. "Let me out! I'll take care of that panther!"

So the turtle went out through the back, quietly approached the panther, and began to bite him until he fled. Once the panther was gone, the two girls left in search of their mother and baby brother. By that evening, they were having dinner together, saving a place of honor for the brave turtle!

The Trickster Oracle

A long time ago, in a faraway kingdom, there was a fortune teller who was often asked to predict future events for the king.

One day, a girl dressed in rags knocked on the door of the king's palace: "I'm a poor orphan," she said. "Can you help me?"

The king welcomed the girl into his home and sent for the fortune teller to ask him what her future held.

The seer discovered that the child was destined to become very beautiful and would bring good luck to whatever house she inhabited. He decided to keep the girl with him, so that he would be the one to benefit from her good fortune.

He quickly came up with a fake prediction and said, "Sire, this girl is a bad omen. In seven days she will turn into a ferocious beast. You must imprison her in a golden box, lock that box in a silver box, and seal them inside an iron box. Then have the boxes taken to the densest part of the forest and leave them there forever."

The king followed his advice to the letter. On the seventh day, he had the little girl brought to the forest.

But as fate would have it, the king of a nearby land was out hunting in that same forest. He had just captured a bear when he heard a muffled cry. He followed the sound and found the iron box. He opened it and was surprised to find another, more precious box inside. The king opened that one too and found a golden chest, the little girl inside.

Amazed, the neighboring king took her to his castle with the gold and silver boxes. He stuffed the terrible bear into the iron box and left them both behind.

That same night, the fortune teller snuck into the forest to retrieve the iron box, quite happy with himself.

He closed all the doors and all the windows so that no one would discover what he'd done. Once he was sure that no one could see him, he opened the iron box. To his surprise, he found not a silver chest, but a frightening and very, very angry bear. The fortune teller tried to escape, but the bear followed him into the woods.

In the end, his prediction had come true: A ferocious beast appeared seven days after the little girl had arrived at the castle.

The Selfish Giant

Once upon a time, there was a giant who decided to go around the world with his ogre friend. While he was away, the children of the village got into the habit of playing in his beautiful garden.

After seven years, the giant returned and immediately chased the children away, building a wall around the garden to keep them out. The disappointed children looked for another place to play, but nowhere else could compare.

Spring finally came. When the giant looked outside, he realized that his garden was bare and snowy while budding trees and flowers covered the meadows beyond his walls.

Even as summer arrived, winter lingered in his garden. The giant fell ill from the cold and spent his days in bed, getting up only to check that the children weren't playing outside of his house.

Autumn came, followed by another winter, and the giant grew increasingly sick and lonely. One day, in early spring, he heard cheerful chirping. It was the most beautiful sound: Finally, the birds had come back to sing in his garden! His heart burst with joy as he looked out into the garden and saw that three children were playing there. Everywhere they went, flowers bloomed and the snow melted.

The giant rushed outside, but instead of chasing the children away, he began tearing down the wall. As the wall slowly crumbled, the giant got his strength back and love filled his heart.

The village children returned to playing in the giant's garden where, from that day on, it was always spring.

The Tortoise and the Monkey

One day, as a turtle was warming himself in the sun on the banks of a river, he noticed that a banana plant was about to be swept away by the current. "I could plant it and harvest its fruit," thought the turtle. He dove into the water to retrieve it. He easily pushed the banana plant to shore, but it was too heavy for him to move on dry land. He went in search of help and soon came across a monkey.

"I found a banana tree in the river and pushed it ashore," the turtle said. "But I can't move it any farther. Will you help me carry it to my garden?"

The monkey agreed, on one condition. "I'll help you, if we then divide the tree in half."

The turtle accepted the deal and the two returned to the river. They dragged the plant out of the water and brought it to the turtle's garden. The turtle asked the monkey to help him dig a deep hole for the plant, but the monkey was tired and didn't want to work anymore. The turtle tried to convince him, saying he would share some of the fruit once it was ripe.

"It'll take too long!" said the monkey. "Let's cut the tree in half now: half for you and half for me, like we agreed."

And that's just what they did. The monkey looked at the two halves and took the upper half with the leaves, since he believed it was better. He ran to plant it in his garden. The turtle was left with the lower half, without leaves, but with all the roots. He dug a nice hole in the ground and planted the stalk carefully.

After some time, the monkey's half turned yellow and died. The turtle's half soon sprouted flowers, which eventually became beautiful bananas. The turtle wanted to harvest them, but since he couldn't climb up the trunk, he asked the monkey for help in exchange for a few bananas.

The monkey easily climbed up the tree. But instead of throwing the bananas down to the turtle, he sat on a branch and ate one banana after another.

When the turtle demanded his share, the monkey said, "You cheated me when we divided the tree, so now I'll be the one to eat all the bananas. If you want, I'll leave you the peels!"

The turtle was beside himself with anger. He walked into the jungle, where he gathered some brambles covered in thorns. Once he got back to his garden, he arranged them around the banana tree and hid to see what would happen. When the monkey had eaten the last banana, he slid joyfully down the stalk, landing in the middle of the brambles. Poked by the thorns, he began howling and hopping about.

The turtle watched the scene, laughing until his sides ached. The monkey heard him. He leaped over to the turtle, flipping him onto his back. The turtle was stuck!

"Now I'll really punish you!" yelled the angry monkey.

But the turtle was quite clever. "Do with me what you wish," he said. "But whatever you do, please don't throw me into the water!"

"That's exactly what I'm going to do!" yelled the monkey. He hurled the turtle into the river. For an instant, the turtle disappeared below the water, but he soon resurfaced, swimming effortlessly.

"Thanks, monkey! You should have known that I'm a great swimmer!" said the turtle. And he swam away to find a new home, with more generous neighbors.

The Parrot
and the Well

Once upon a time, in the African savanna, there lived a leopard who went to the watering hole multiple times a day to escape the heat and drink some water. The watering hole was big, but it was also the only one around. Many animals flocked to it: elephants, zebras, lions, and even a parrot, who always complained, saying that the water was dirty and tasted bad.

The other animals silently tolerated his outbursts. One day, however, the leopard got tired of his babbling and asked him to quit complaining.

"You know how to fly," he said. "Why don't you go to other watering holes that are farther away or fly to a river, where the running water is fresh and clean?"

The elephant seconded that. "Yeah, why don't you leave this muddy water for us, if you hate it so much?"

The parrot replied, "The water isn't good, but in this heat I wouldn't make it to the river, so I have to make do."

Then he turned to the leopard and said, "You're so fast, you could reach the river easily. Why don't you do it?"

The leopard said, "The difference between you and me is that I choose to stay without complaint. You, on the other hand, just whine all the time!"

He then cunningly added, "Actually, I think your whining is what's making the water so dirty! Even the water has feelings, and if it doesn't feel appreciated, it becomes rotten and you can't drink it anymore."

The parrot, struck by the leopard's words, stopped his complaining. But the other animals decided he had to leave.

The elephant stepped forward and said to the parrot, "We don't want you here anymore. Leave, and maybe the water will be as good as it used to be!"

Even though the water had never been as good as they claimed, the parrot had no choice but to fly away. The heat got the better of him before he could reach the river.

The parrot had failed to understand one important thing: It is best to accept the things which you cannot change, and to try to see the silver lining of every situation. After all, things can always get worse!

The Monkey and the Crocodile

A long time ago, a monkey and a crocodile were the best of friends, spending all of their time having fun together. When they were hungry, the monkey would climb up a tree and throw the tastiest fruit to the crocodile.

But one day, the crocodile decided she would rather eat the monkey's heart, so she devised a plan. She turned to her friend and said, "I always feel like I'm your guest here. I would like to return the favor. What do you say to lunch at my place?"

The monkey wanted to accept, though there was one problem. "How will I get there? You live on an island in the middle of the river and I can't swim!"

"I'll carry you on my back!" the crocodile said.

The monkey climbed on the crocodile's back, and she swam quickly toward the island she called home. They were in the middle of the river when the crocodile began crying inconsolably.

"What's wrong, friend?" asked the monkey.

The crocodile said, "My son is very sick and the doctor says he'll die if I don't bring him a monkey heart to eat. Would you help us and give him a piece of yours?"

The monkey realized what the crocodile was plotting, and said, "Of course, but we left so quickly that I forgot my heart at home! Let's go back for it!"

The crocodile swam the monkey back to shore. Once they arrived, the monkey climbed up his tree and when he was safe, began to sing.

"I once had a lying crocodile as a friend. And now, if I live to tell the tale, it's because I'll never walk on the ground again."

The disappointed and hungry crocodile returned home, but she didn't give up on the idea of eating a monkey heart. The next day, she waited in the meadow where the monkey liked to nap. Once he fell asleep, she'd grab him with her powerful jaws.

The monkey, however, was quite clever. When he went to the meadow, he found a bit of land that was higher up, so he could see everything around him. When he saw something move in the grass, he said, "Field, my friend, is the traitor crocodile hidden in the grass? If we're all clear, let me know by yelling 'uh-huh'!"

The crocodile yelled out, "Uh-huh!"

The monkey burst into thunderous laughter and fled, leaving the crocodile high and dry. And what a pity—their friendship was ruined forever!

Rumpelstiltskin

Once upon a time, there was a miller who was poor but had a beautiful daughter. One day, he told the king that the young woman could spin straw into gold. The king called her to his castle, where he locked her in a room full of straw. He gave her a spinning wheel and a reel and said, "If you don't spin all this hay into gold by morning, it's off with your head!"

The poor girl knew she could never do as the king asked, and she began to cry. Suddenly, the door opened and a little imp appeared. He asked her why she was crying.

The girl explained, and the man said, "What would you give me if I did the job for you?"

"I can give you my necklace," she replied.

The man took the necklace and got to work. By dawn, all the straw in the room had been spun into gold thread.

The king was quite happy, but he wanted more. He led her to a larger room, also full of straw, and told her he would cut off her head if she didn't turn all the straw into gold by morning. Once again, the girl sobbed in despair, and once again the imp appeared.

"What will you give me if I turn all this straw into gold?"

"My ring," answered the maiden.

The man took the ring and got to work. By morning, all the straw had been turned into gold. But once again, the king was greedy. He brought the miller's daughter to an even larger room, full of straw, and said, "Spin all this straw into gold and, if you do, I'll marry you and make you queen."

Like the last two nights, the imp came to her and asked, "What will you give me if I spin all this straw to gold?"

"I have nothing to give," answered the maiden.

"Well then, you must promise that when you are queen, you'll give me your first-born child."

Without much of a choice, the girl accepted. The following morning, the room was full of gold instead of straw. The king kept his promise and married her.

A year later, the queen gave birth to a healthy baby boy. When the imp came to claim what had been promised to him, the young woman begged him not to take her child, offering him endless riches.

The imp gave her one chance to win back her son. "You have three days. If you can find out my name in that time, you can keep the child."

The queen tossed and turned all night, trying to remember every name she had ever heard. She repeated them all the next morning when the imp came to her, but none of them were right.

With two days left, she sent her messengers to gather all the names there were, even the strangest ones. She recited them to the imp the next morning, but she still hadn't managed to find his name.

One the third day, one of her messengers said, "I didn't find any new names, but at the base of a mountain I saw a small house. In front of it there was a big bonfire, and a silly-looking man danced around it, yelling:

"Tonight, tonight, my plans I make,

Tomorrow, tomorrow, the baby I take.

The queen will never win the game,

For Rumpelstiltskin is my name!"

Shortly after, the imp appeared before the queen.

"So, what is my name?" he asked.

The queen paused a moment, then said, "Is your name Rumpelstiltskin?"

"The devil told you, I'm sure of it!" the imp yelled. He ran away, never to be seen again.

The Vain Giraffe

In Africa, at the edges of a large forest, there lived a beautiful giraffe who was taller than all the other giraffes. All of the other animals sung her praises and soon the giraffe become vain and snobby. She no longer respected anyone and never offered to help a soul. She grew selfish, collecting the food from the highest branches that no one else could reach and refusing to share it.

One day, Mr. Monkey decided it was time the giraffe learned an important lesson. Flattering her with words of admiration, he led her to a large palm tree, telling her that she should collect the dates that were up on the highest branches, as they were sure to be the sweetest.

The vain giraffe's neck was very long, but as hard as she tried, she still couldn't reach the dates. So the monkey disrespectfully jumped on her back and climbed up her neck until he stood on her head, easily grabbing the fruit.

Back on the ground, the monkey spoke to the giraffe, who looked at him in shock. "It's true that your height gives you an advantage, but even you cannot live without the help of others."

The giraffe learned her lesson and she began to share what she didn't need and show respect for all the other animals in the forest.

The Daughter of the Moon and the Sun

There was once a young hunter who lived in a land far, far away. Every day, his mother told him to avoid the dragon's mountain. He was a dangerous creature who had killed all who had gone to his lair.

But food grew scarce in the hunter's village and the people were hungry while the dragon's mountain was rich with food. One day, the hunter's betrothed said, "If you truly love me, today you'll hunt on the dragon's mountain."

The young man agreed. When he reached the mountain, he heard a loud roar. The earth began to shake. A huge dragon appeared, with seven tails, seven heads, and seven huge mouths that breathed snaking tongues of fire. As the dragon approached, the hunter shot his arrows, striking the beast. Yet the dragon's scales weren't even scratched! "You have no chance! I'll defeat you, like all the others who came before you," the dragon said.

The hunter replied, "I know, but I must ask you a favor. Let me go so I can say goodbye to my mother. I promise I'll return."

Surprisingly, the monster agreed.

The young man went to his mother and told her what had happened. The woman begged her son not to return, but the hunter was adamant. He hugged her, then went

to his fiancée to see her one last time. She too begged him not to go back, but the young man didn't give in: He had given the dragon his word!

So the young maiden said, "Well then, I'll come with you!"

The dragon appeared once they reached the mountain. He laughed. "It's my lucky day! Today there are two of you!"

But the young woman faced him and said, "You are mistaken. Today will be the worst day of your life. You'll return to the bowels of the Earth, where you belong, because this mountain is for men!"

The dragon reared up on its hind legs and got ready to burn her with its flames, but the girl stopped him with just her stare. Incredulous, the dragon asked her, "Who are you, with such incredible powers?"

"I'm the daughter of the moon and the sun. I'm the drop from the sky that falls on every corner of the world, bringing joy to the good and punishing the bad. I'm the water that makes hills and fields fertile. I am the daughter of the moon and the sun!"

The dragon, defeated, sank forever into the belly of the Earth. From that day forth, people were able to hunt safely on the mountain once again.

The Ball of Light

When the Earth was first created, many eons ago, the land of the Inuit was always dark.

One day, an old raven flew over their land and, surprised by the eternal darkness, told them that other places had warm, sunny days, with light that shone like thousands of lamps lit up at once.

So, the Inuit asked the raven to give them that sort of light, the kind that comes from a thousand lamps. The bird was old and tired, but he decided to help them and left in search of the light.

He flew for days on end until, almost out of strength, he saw a faint glow on the horizon.

When the raven realized he was flying in broad daylight, he knew he had reached the Land of Light.

But how could he bring the light to the Inuit?

As he sat thinking on a branch, a little girl with a snow-white fur cape came to fill her bucket with water from a stream. The raven magically turned into a speck of dust and hid in the bristles of the girl's cape. She brought him back to her family's house.

The house was warm and welcoming. A woman was sewing a fur coat while the old head of the village was warming up before the fire. A little boy was playing with some bone figurines on the floor. The raven flew into the child's ear and began to tickle him. Annoyed, the little boy began to cry. The old man walked over to see what was wrong.

The raven whispered, "Tell him you want to play with a Ball of Light."

At the request of his grandson, the old man went to the box in which he kept the Balls of Light, took out a small one, tied it with a string, and gave it to the child.

The raven once again tickled the boy's ear, making him cry again. He whispered that the boy should say he wanted to play with the Ball of Light outdoors.

The old man took the boy to the front yard and then returned to the warmth of the house.

Once the child was finally alone, the speck of dust turned back into the raven. He cut the string that bound the Ball of Light, grabbed it with his talons, and flew to the land of the Inuit.

The raven finally arrived at his destination, exhausted by the long journey. The Inuit ran out of their homes, but were disappointed to find that the darkness had not disappeared.

Then, the raven dropped the Ball of Light, which shattered into a million pieces and chased the darkness of night away.

Only then could the Inuit people see far away and admire the world around them. They hunted and fished for many hours a day, so that they never went hungry again.

They thanked the raven, who warned them, "I was only able to get a small Ball of Light, so you will only have light for half the year."

But the Inuit were happy anyway. Never again would they spend an entire year in darkness!

The Ridiculous Wishes

Once upon a time, there was a poor woodcutter who was tired of his difficult life. He often said that not one of his wishes had ever been fulfilled. One day, while he worked in the woods, Jupiter himself appeared before him. Frightened, the man hastened to retract all his complaints, worried that he would be punished by the god.

"Fear not," responded Jupiter. "I have heard your complaints and I promise to grant the first three wishes you can come up with. Think about what might make you happy, but think long and hard before speaking. Your fate depends on your wishes."

Jupiter returned to Mount Olympus and the woodcutter headed home.

"It would be a pity," he thought to himself, "to decide with haste. I'll speak to my wife and ask for her advice."

When he crossed the threshold to his hut, he called for his wife. "Come here and rejoice! For we are rich. All we have to do is make a wish!"

He told her what had happened. Many wishes ran through his wife's mind, but she knew that they had to be careful.

"My dear," she said. "Let's not ruin the opportunity with our impatience. Let's sleep on it and decide tomorrow."

"Alright!" said her husband. "Now fetch me some more wine, please."

When she returned with the wine, the man exclaimed, "I wish we had a delicious loaf of bread to eat before that lovely fire."

As soon as he had pronounced those words, his stunned wife saw a giant loaf of bread creep out of the corner of the fireplace. It didn't take long for her to figure out that it had been summoned by her husband's wish, and she began to yell at the careless woodcutter. "How could you wish for bread when you could ask for an empire, gold, pearls, rubies, diamonds as big as hazelnuts, and dresses fit for a queen?"

"I have been a fool," he answered. "I wasted a wish; I'll do better next time."

But his wife continued yelling and insulting him. At his wit's end, the woodcutter said,

"Curse that bread and the moment I wished for it! With all of your complaints, I wish the gods would just hang it from your nose!"

As soon as he said that, the woman found herself with the bread in place of her nose. The poor man began to fret, and thought perhaps he should wait before making any more wishes. He could become king, but how would his wife feel is she had to appear before crowds of people with bread for a nose? He asked her which she preferred: to become queen and keep the nose, or to remain a poor woodcutter's wife with the nose she had before.

The woman thought about it carefully and ultimately decided she'd rather have her old nose back. And so, the woodcutter remained what he was. He never became king and never filled his home with bags of money, but he was happy to have used his last wish to get his wife's lovely nose back.

The Vain Bat

One cold winter evening, a shivering young bat sought shelter in a cave. He couldn't seem to warm up, even as he curled up and wrapped himself in his large wings. He began to cry out of desperation.

"It's so cold," he said. "I'll never make it through winter."

His cries grew louder and quickly spread throughout the land, from the depths of the earth to the sky. A mighty eagle heard his cries and flew to the cave to see who was making all the fuss. When he saw the poor little bat, he asked him what was the matter.

"I'm so, so cold and I can't warm up," answered the bat.

The eagle looked at him, confused, and said, "But other birds don't cry as you do, and they don't complain. What's the matter with you?"

The bat explained, "The other birds, as you can easily see, have warm, soft feathers that protect them from the cold. But I'm nearly bald and I'm certainly not suited to surviving the cold of winter!"

The eagle, who was quite wise, understood why the little creature was so worried and promised to help him. After all, it was the first time the bat had to endure the harsh winter.

He flew out of the cave and asked all the other birds he met to donate one of their

feathers to the poor bat. He returned with the feathers in his beak and gave them to the surprised bat, who began attaching them to his body. When he was finished, he had transformed into a beautiful bird with thick, colorful plumage. Without stopping to thank the eagle, he took flight and left the cave.

The more time passed, the more proud and vain the bat became. He spent entire days looking at his reflection in ponds and lakes, and didn't pay attention to anyone else. Annoyed by his behavior, the birds in the area went to the eagle, who promised them that he would take care of the matter.

He found the bat and told him, "I've received lots of complaints from the other birds about your haughty, rude behavior. What do you say to that?"

"What do you want me to say?" answered the bat with disdain. "They're just jealous of my beautiful plumage!"

The eagle then understood that there was only one thing to do. He took flight, called all the birds to him, and said they could take back the feathers they had so generously given the bat.

In a flash, the bat found himself without feathers, bare and exposed. He was so ashamed that he only left his cave at night, when the darkness sheltered him from the stares of other animals.

The Spirit in the Glass Bottle

Once upon a time there was a woodcutter who had worked hard and managed to save a small amount of money to send his son to school. The boy went to the city to begin his education. He learned a great deal, but soon the money ran out and he had to return home. His father was ashamed and disappointed, but the boy said, "Don't worry about me; I'll manage. And besides, it's time that I help you."

One day, the two walked into the forest to chop wood. When the father stopped to rest, the boy decided to go for a stroll.

When he reached a giant oak tree, a little voice called out to him. "Please! Help me get out of here!" the voice said.

The young man looked around and found a glass bottle in the dirt. The voice seemed to be coming from there! He removed the cork and a spirit came out. It quickly grew to an enormous size.

"If you're expecting a reward for freeing me, you'll be greatly disappointed. I'm the powerful Mercurius. I've been trapped in that bottle as punishment, and that's just what you'll get for freeing me!"

The boy wracked his brain and said, "Wait! How can I be sure? For all I know, it was someone else's magic that allowed you to be small enough to fit into the tiny bottle."

The spirit laughed and effortlessly returned to the bottle. The clever boy immediately closed it, leaving Mercurius where he found him.

The spirit begged to be let out, promising the boy all the riches he could want. Eventually, the student decided to set him free.

Coming out of his glass prison, Mercurius gave the boy a piece of cloth, explaining, "One end will heal any wound you rub it against and the other will turn steel or iron into silver."

He then disappeared and the young man walked back to his father. He tested the gift, rubbing his ax with the rag. The ax turned into silver. When he got back to work,

the ax broke in two at the first blow. The father was dismayed: Now he didn't even have the ax anymore! He sent his son to sell it at the market to regain some money.

The boy went to a goldsmith in the village and showed him the ax. The goldsmith gave him three hundred coins for the silver. Once he came back home, the boy gave the money to his father, explaining how he got it. Their problems were solved and his father could finally rest.

The boy returned to school and, thanks to the magical cloth's ability to heal all wounds, he became the wealthiest, most respected doctor in the land.

Beauty and the Beast

Once upon a time, there was a young, selfish prince who lived in a wonderful castle. One winter night, a beggar asked the prince for a place to shelter from the cold. He offered a rose as payment, but the prince refused and tried to send him away. To the prince's surprise the beggar was a powerful fairy in disguise, and he cast a spell so that the prince's appearance reflected his beastly manners. The spell would only be broken if the prince could make someone love him before the enchanted rose withered.

The prince's subjects were intimidated by his frightening new appearance, and the castle emptied until only the prince remained. Alone with his thoughts, he soon realized the error of his ways.

Years later, a merchant came to his castle to escape a terrible snowstorm. He spent a comfortable night in the castle without laying eyes on his host, but as he was leaving, he saw a flowerbed with a beautiful red rose at its center that his daughter, Bella, would love. As soon as he touched the flower, he heard a voice behind him. "Is this how you repay me for saving you from the storm?"

"Forgive me, I beg you. I just wanted to bring a gift to my daughter, who loves roses," pleaded the merchant.

"I will spare you, but only if your daughter comes to live with me." The last thing the merchant wanted was to give up his youngest daughter, but he told his children what happened when he arrived at home and Bella set off for the castle.

Despite the merchant's fears, the Beast proved to be a true gentleman and a perfect host. Soon Bella was no longer afraid of the Beast and grew to truly care for him.

Despite all the attention she was getting, Bella was quite sad.

The Beast realized that Bella was homesick. Her happiness was the most important thing to the Beast, so even though the rose had started to lose its petals, he agreed to

let Bella return to her family for a while. Bella was reunited with her father, but her sisters, jealous of her luxurious life in the castle, tried to keep her in their modest house beyond the time the Beast had granted her.

One night, the fairy who had cursed the prince appeared in her dreams and revealed the spell he had cast on the rose. He showed Bella the rose as it was now, with its last petal about to fall. Bella awoke with a start, said goodbye to her father, and rode to the castle, where she found the weak and dying Beast.

"Don't leave me! I love you!" she cried, just as the enchanted rose lost its last petal. The spell was broken and the Beast turned back into a prince. With the curse broken, the castle began to fill with people once again. Bella was able to visit her father often with her husband, the prince, by her side.

The Tale of the Hummingbird

One day, an awful fire broke out in the forest, forcing all of the animals to flee as the fire destroyed everything in its path. They sought shelter in a great river, but the flames soon reached even the river.

While the animals debated what to do, a small hummingbird dove into the river and grabbed a drop of water in her beak. She paid no mind to the heat as she poured the water droplet over the smoke-filled forest. The fire continued raging, pushed along by the wind. Still, the hummingbird didn't give up. She kept diving into the water to collect the small droplets that she dropped onto the flames. Her actions didn't go unnoticed.

"What are you doing?" a lion asked.

The bird replied, "I'm trying to put out the fire!"

The lion laughed. "You're so small! You'll never stop the flames."

The other animals joined the lion in mocking the hummingbird, but she paid them no mind and continued trying to save the forest. A baby elephant who had been hiding between his mom's legs, plunged his trunk into the river and sucked up as much

water as possible. He sprayed it on a bush that was about to burn, keeping the fire away from it. Then a young pelican left his parents in the middle of the river and filled his big beak with water before taking flight. He dropped a waterfall onto a tree and kept it from being devoured by the flames.

Influenced by those good examples, the other young animals did their best to put out the fire that had reached the banks of the river. Forgetting age-old rivalries, the lion cub and the antelope, the leopard and the monkey, the eagle and the hare fought side by side to stop the fire. The adult animals saw them working together and, ashamed, began to help their children.

With the arrival of reinforcements, the fire was tamed by the time evening fell. Finally safe, yet dirty and tired, all the animals came together to celebrate their victory over the fire.

The lion called the little hummingbird over and apologized. "Your tiny drop of water was the most important one of all," he said. "You showed us that if we do what we can and work together, we can solve even our greatest problems."

Bohra the Kangaroo

Long ago, in the days when kangaroos walked on all fours like dogs, night brought a darkness that veiled even the moon and stars from the sky. One day Bohra the kangaroo, who preferred to eat at night, grew tired of the darkness. He grabbed the dark sky and rolled it up like a carpet so that the stars and the moon shined through the night. The kangaroo was happy: Finally he could see what he was eating and walk around confidently.

One night, he saw lots of fires and heard many voices singing. Curious, he walked towards the sound and saw a group of people whose bodies were painted with symbols that Bohra had never seen before. They were dancing in a circle, beating the rhythm with a boomerang.

Watching them, Bohra felt the uncontrollable desire to start dancing as well. Balancing with his tail, he stood up on his hind legs and joined the circle. The men stopped dancing and watched in wonder and terror as Bohra tried to imitate them.

After a while, the men decided to make tails of their own with braids of brushwood and grass. They attached the tails to their belts, and began dancing like the kangaroo to the amusement of all.

When the party was over, they gathered to discuss Bohra's fate. They decided that they wouldn't kill him, but that they would punish him for taking part in their ceremony without invitation. Bohra was put under a spell that made him walk on his two hind legs, like kangaroos do today.

To remember the occasion, local men still wear fake tails and repeat the dance of the kangaroo during festive ceremonies.

Maui and the Sun

Long ago, there was a demigod named Maui. He was clever and tricky, but he respected mankind and used his trickiness to make their lives easier.

The sun did not seem to share Maui's respect for humanity. The sun ran too fast and shone too bright. The days were short and unbearably hot. It was impossible to get work done, and people went hungry as the fruit was unable to ripen in the trees. Many complained about the sun's thoughtlessness.

One night, Maui went to visit his mother Hina. She had her own complaints against the sun.

"Another day is gone, and the sun left before my kapa cloth could dry properly," Hina said.

Many went to Hina for cloth that they could use to make new clothes, but the short days didn't allow her enough time to finish her work. Hearing this, Maui was determined to get the sun to slow down and control his power. He told his mother what he planned to do.

"Are you sure that you're strong enough to match the sun?" his mother asked.

"Yes," he said.

"Then you must go to see your grandmother." Every morning, the sun stopped to eat the bananas that Maui's grandmother cooked for him. It would be the best place to catch him.

"Go to the top of Mt. Haleakala, where the large wiliwili tree stands, and wait for your grandmother to make a fire. Then take the bananas she leaves and wait for her to find you. When she does, tell her that you are my son. She'll give you what you need to complete your task," Hina said. She gave her son fifteen ropes of strong fiber and sent him on his way.

Maui traveled to the top of the mountain as his mother suggested. He crouched near the wiliwili tree until his grandmother appeared with her bananas. Maui quickly stole the bananas when his grandmother wasn't looking and hid himself nearby.

His grandmother searched for the missing bananas and soon found Maui.

"Who are you, and why have you come here?" his grandmother asked.

"I am Hina's son, and I have come to capture the sun," Maui replied.

His grandmother agreed to help him. She gave Maui one more rope to add to the fifteen his mother had given him. Maui's grandmother told him to make lassos of all sixteen. "When the sun appears, use them to catch his legs and tie them to the tree so he can't move."

Maui returned to his hiding place by the tree and waited for the sun to appear. When its first ray came over the mountainside, Maui caught it in his lasso. The sun fought against him, and before he could tie the rope to the tree, the ray had broken off. Maui tried again, but the sun fought him each time, and each time another strong ray broke from the sun.

Finally, Maui managed to snare the sun using his final lasso.

"Why have you captured me?" the sun asked.

"Because you have no respect for the people below you," Maui replied. "You move so quickly that fruit cannot grow and kapa cannot dry. Your strongest rays make the heat unbearable. Swear that you'll slow down and control your rays or I'll keep you as my captive."

"My strongest rays have already broken, and I will slow down," the sun agreed.

From that day on, the days were cooler, the sun moved more slowly across the sky, and the people were content.

The Emperor's New Clothes

Many years ago, there was an emperor who cared a lot about the beauty of his clothes. One day, two swindlers showed up at the royal court. They claimed to be famous weavers who could create clothes made with fabric that had an incredible quality: They were invisible to people who weren't fit for the office they held or who, quite simply, weren't very smart.

"If I had those clothes, I could easily tell wise men from fools and find out who isn't right for the role I've assigned them," thought the emperor.

So he gave the men a generous advance payment. They quickly set up two looms, and asked the king for the most precious silk thread and the finest gold in the kingdom. They hid the items in their bags and pretended to weave on empty looms.

"I wonder how things are going with my fabric," thought the emperor one day. He decided to send his trusted viceroy, unquestionably honest and quite intelligent, to check on the two men.

The viceroy walked into the room where the two scoundrels were pretending to work. "My goodness!" he thought. "I don't see anything! Does that make me stupid? What if I'm unfit for my job? I certainly can't go back and say I don't see the fabric. I'll just say it's marvelous!"

A few days later, the emperor sent one of his best officers to inspect the weavers' work. The high-ranking officer fell into the same trap. He began to doubt himself when he realized he couldn't see the fabric.

"But, I'm no fool!" he thought. "Well then, it must mean I'm not cut out for my job. In any case, I'll just tell the emperor that the fabric is incredible!"

Intrigued, the emperor wanted to see the fabric for himself. Accompanied by his most trusted men, he went to the two fake weavers.

"It's beautiful, isn't it Your Majesty?" they all exclaimed, thinking that the others were able to see the fabric.

"I don't see anything!" thought the emperor. "Could I be stupid? Or incapable of being emperor?"

Distressed by these thoughts, he said, "Wow! They're magnificent!"

They all advised him to wear the clothing made from that fabric during the great procession he would soon lead.

The evening before the day of the festivities, the two swindlers pretended to cut the fabric from the loom. They cut the air with large shears, sewed nothing with a needle and no thread, then exclaimed, "Here you go, your clothes are ready!"

Raising their arms in the air as if holding something, they said, "Here are the trousers! Here's the tunic! Here's the cloak! They're light as air!"

The emperor stripped down and those tricksters pretended to put the clothes on him, one by one.

"Your Majesty, you look absolutely divine," his advisors said.

"They really look good on me, don't they?" said the emperor. He walked over to the mirror, as if admiring the new outfit.

The next day, the emperor took his place at the start of the procession. As he passed by, the crowd praised the emperor's clothing. No one wanted to admit they saw nothing, afraid that others would think they were foolish or unfit for their job.

"But he doesn't have any clothes!" a child yelled.

The people began to whisper, then even yell, "The emperor has no clothes!"

The emperor shuddered, knowing they were right. "But the procession must go on," he thought. So he held his head high and walked proudly until the ceremony was over.

Hop-o'-My-Thumb

There once was a woodcutter with seven children. The youngest child was only the size of a man's thumb, and so they called him Hop-o'-My-Thumb. Time passed, but Hop-o'-My-Thumb didn't grow a single inch, though he was very clever.

One year, there was a terrible famine in his village and the woodcutter had to set out in search of work, leaving his sons in the care of a distant relative. But she turned out to be a very wicked woman and, when the boys' father left, she abandoned them in the woods.

Luckily, Hop-o'-My-Thumb, hidden on the mantelpiece, heard the woman talking about her plans and had come up with one of his own! The following day, he gathered a handful of pebbles before they set out to the woods and dropped them along their path. He and his brothers used the stones to find their way home.

She tried again the next day, taking the children even farther into the woods. This time, Hop-o'-My-Thumb had only managed to collect a few crumbs. He dropped them on the trail, but they were eaten by birds. He and his brothers had no idea how to return to the house.

When the brothers realized what had happened, they began to cry, but Hop-o'-My-Thumb reassured them. He had seen another house nearby.

When they knocked on the door, a woman let all seven brothers in, warning them that the house belonged to a terrible ogre. Shortly after, the ogre returned and realized there were intruders in his home. As the ogre began searching for them, Hop-o'-My-Thumb and his brothers ran into the woods.

Enraged, the ogre chased them, but Hop-o'-My-Thumb set a trap: He pulled a long rope between two trees and waited for the ogre to trip, sending him tumbling into a nearby ravine. The children rejoiced and returned to the house to tell the kind woman what happened. She was so happy that the ogre was gone that she gave the children the gold the ogre had hidden in the cellar.

Hop-o'-My-Thumb and his brothers returned home, where they found their father, just back from his travels. He gave them a big hug, promising he wouldn't leave ever again.

"Don't worry. You won't need to," said Hop-o'-My-Thumb as he poured hundreds of shiny coins onto the floor.

The Lion and the Mouse

While a lion was sleeping under a tree, a few field mice were playing on a branch above. One of them tripped and landed on the lion, waking him up. With a quick leap, the lion grabbed the mouse, determined to rip him to shreds for the rude awakening. The small rodent trembled with fear and begged for forgiveness, promising to help the lion for the rest of his life.

The lion smiled. How could such a small creature ever be helpful to him, the biggest, scariest animal in the jungle? Still, he decided to let the mouse go.

Just a few days later, the lion fell into a trap set by hunters and couldn't get out no matter what he tried. He was stuck! The mouse, hearing the echoes of his frightened roars, came to his aid.

The mouse gnawed at the ropes that trapped the lion until he was free. The lion lept out of the trap and the mouse followed after him. The mouse said, "You once laughed at me because you thought I could never be helpful to you. Now you know that, no matter how large or small, we all have something to offer!"

The Old Woman in the Woods

A poor servant girl was once traveling through the forest with her lord and lady when their carriage was attacked by bandits. The young girl escaped, but she was lost and alone in the woods. That night, as she laid down to sleep under a large oak tree, a pretty white dove landed next to her, holding a small golden key in its beak. As it gave her the key, it said, "This key unlocks a small door hidden in the trunk of this tree. If you go inside, you'll find plenty of food and drink."

The young maiden followed the dove's instructions and ate until she was full before getting ready to sleep on the ground. Before she had settled in, the dove gave her a second golden key and said, "Open the tree you see over there and you'll find a comfortable bed."

The young woman spent a peaceful night in the softest bed she had ever slept in.

The following morning, the dove reappeared with a new key and directed her to another tree nearby. It said, "Open the tree and you'll find some clothes."

The clothes were worthy of a princess!

The servant girl lived for a while in the forest, and the dove returned every day to take care of her. One morning, the bird said, "I need to ask you a favor."

"Anything at all!" she replied.

"I'll accompany you to a house where an old woman lives," the dove said. "No matter what she tells you, you must not speak to her. On the right you will see a door; it will lead to a room with a large table in the center, holding rings of every kind. Take only the simplest one, then run outside and bring it to me."

The servant girl did as she was told, but when she got to the room she didn't see the ring. Out of the corner of her eye, however, she saw the old lady running outside, carrying a cage.

The young girl ran to stop her and grabbed it. Inside the cage, there was a bird with the ring she had been searching for in its beak.

The girl took it and ran to the oak tree. Suddenly, the branches became two arms and the tree turned into a handsome prince.

"My dear, by taking the ring you have freed me from the old woman's cruel spell. Years ago, she turned me into a tree out of envy, allowing me only two hours a day to fly freely in the form of a dove."

The servant girl fell in love with the prince who had been so generous to her even through his own hardship, and the prince fell in love with her as well. They married and lived happily ever after.

Jack and the Beanstalk

There was once a young boy named Jack whose mother asked him to sell their cow at the market. The cow was the last thing they owned that was worth much money, so his mother told him to sell her for a good price.

On the way there, Jack came across a merchant who offered him a magic bean in exchange for the cow. Jack accepted, but when he returned home and gave the bean to his mother, she was so mad that she threw the bean out the window.

The next morning, they were surprised to find that a beanstalk had grown in their garden overnight. It was so tall that it reached the clouds. Jack decided to climb it.

He reached the top and saw a castle far off in the distance. Curious, he walked over to it, crossing a drawbridge and entering a huge hall. At the end of the hall, there was a large armchair that held a giant ogre, fast asleep.

Frightened, Jack hid behind a curtain, but he peeked out to keep the ogre in sight. The ogre was surrounded by bags of gold and held a hen in his lap. As Jack watched, the hen laid two golden eggs.

"If only I could bring that hen home to my mother . . ." Jack thought.

Just as Jack finished gathering enough courage to move, the ogre woke up.

He sniffed the air and said, "Fee-fi-fo-fum, I smell the blood of an Englishman! Be he alive, or be he dead, I'll grind his bones to make my bread!"

The ogre got up. Jack leapt and grabbed the hen. He held her tightly and ran out of the castle, but the hen squawked so loudly that the ogre heard and chased after the boy.

Jack reached the top of the beanstalk and descended as quickly as he could. The ogre grabbed the plant to follow after him.

When Jack reached the ground, he grabbed his ax and chopped at the beanstalk until the plant gave way, taking the ogre to the ground and crushing him beneath it. Jack's mom heard a thud and ran out from the kitchen.

Jack explained what happened, proudly showing her the lucky hen and the golden eggs. The little family never went hungry again.

Donkeyskin

Once upon a time, there was a king who had many precious riches, including a donkey that turned straw to gold with a touch of its hoof. Yet of all his riches, the king treasured his wife the most.

One day, the queen fell ill and even the king's best doctors couldn't cure her. Inconsolable, the king refused to remarry. Instead, he decided to offer his daughter's hand in marriage to his wisest courtier and let her take the throne.

However, the princess realized her future husband was a cruel, ruthless man. She made unreasonable demands in order to delay the wedding. First, she asked her father to give her three dresses: one as golden as the sun, the other as silver as the moon, and the third as brilliant as the stars. When the dresses were ready, the princess tried to prevent the wedding altogether.

"I want a cape made from the hide of your magic donkey," she said, sure that the king would never sacrifice his precious animal. Yet the king did as she requested.

With no other options, the princess fled. She folded her new dresses until they fit into a walnut shell. Then, she covered herself in soot, disguised herself in the donkey cape, and left the castle.

The princess made her way to a farm, where she agreed to work in their kitchen in exchange for a small storeroom to live in. The other workers called her Donkeyskin after her cape, which she always wore outside of her room.

One day, while sitting next to a fountain, the princess saw her reflection in the water. She looked so dirty and neglected that she decided to dedicate one day a week to taking care of herself. She tried on each of her beautiful dresses in the privacy of her room.

Months later, a prince stopped at the farm for lunch and wandered around while he waited for his meal to be prepared. He found a small door at the end of a corridor and, finding it was locked, he peeked in through the keyhole. The princess was on the other side of the door, wearing the dress the color of the sun. She looked so beautiful that the prince fell in love at first sight.

Even after he'd returned home, the prince was unable to get the girl he'd seen out of his mind. He summoned the owner of the farm to the castle and asked him about the girl who lived in his storeroom. Incredulous, the owner told him that only a servant girl lived in the storeroom. She was ugly and dirty, but knew how to make delicious cakes. The prince insisted that he had to try one.

Donkeyskin made the cake as requested, not noticing as a fine golden ring that she never took off fell into the batter. Eventually, the ring ended up on the prince's plate. The young man recognized it immediately, remembering the ring from the brief glimpse he'd gotten of the beautiful girl on the farm. So, he said to his mother, "This ring belongs to the woman I love, and will only fit her finger."

The queen summoned every young woman in the kingdom to try on the ring. They came in droves, but no one managed to slip the tiny ring on her finger.

"Was the girl who made the cake also summoned?" asked the prince. He ordered that she be brought to the palace. When Donkeyskin heard the prince's pages knock at her door, she put on the dress that was the color of the moon and put her usual cape on over it.

Once she got to the royal court, she slipped the ring on her finger, let the cape fall to the ground, and revealed herself in all her beauty. The prince recognized her and asked her to marry him on the spot. Donkeyskin told him her story and explained that she couldn't marry without her father's approval. The king was invited to court. When he saw his daughter, the king wept with joy and agreed to the marriage, which was celebrated that same day.

Diamonds and Toads

A widow had two daughters. The older one was like her in looks and character:
Both were so mean and proud that it was impossible to talk with either of them. The
younger one was loved by all for her kindness and her beauty. Her mother treated
her with contempt, forcing her to do chores around the house without rest. Every day,
the younger daughter had to fetch enough water from the spring to fill a heavy clay
pitcher. However, even that difficult task didn't bother her. She used the errand
to spend a few minutes enjoying the silence of the forest.

One cold winter morning, as the girl filled the pitcher, an old peasant woman
wrapped in ragged clothes approached and asked her for something to drink.

"Of course," replied the girl, holding the jug so the woman could drink from it.
Then, seeing that the old woman was shivering from the cold, she offered her cloak.

"Thank you, but I cannot accept it. You have already been too kind," the woman
replied. Her voice and appearance began to change.

The girl's jaw dropped as she watched the old peasant woman transform into
a beautiful woman with eyes and hair the color of ice.

"Who are you?" the girl asked.

"A fairy, my dear. I've come to show my sisters that kindness still exists in the
world. You're living proof of it. Because of your kind heart, I want to give you a gift:
For every word you speak, a flower or precious jewel will fall from your mouth."

When the girl got home, she was harshly reprimanded by her mother for being late.

"I'm sorry . . .", she began to say, but before she could finish, three roses, two pearls, and four diamonds came out of her mouth.

"Where did you find these jewels?" asked her mother, collecting them from the ground. The girl told her of the fairy, a cascade of rubies tumbling from her mouth as she spoke.

Her mother called for her eldest daughter. "You must go to the spring! Find the old woman there and be kind to her so that you can receive the same gift as your sister."

The girl put on her warmest clothes, took a silver pitcher, and grudgingly left the house. Once she got to the spring, she saw a wonderfully dressed woman appear out of the woods with eyes and hair the color of ice. The woman approached and asked the girl for something to drink.

As she looked nothing like the old woman her mother had mentioned, the girl scoffed and said, "If you want water, get it yourself!"

The fairy responded, "Before you leave, I want to give you a gift that's just right for you. For every word you speak, a toad will come out of your mouth."

As soon as she got back home, her mother asked, "Well? How did it go?"

"It . . .", as she began to speak, toads jumped out of her mouth.

"This is all your fault," yelled the mother, lunging at her kind younger daughter. The girl was forced to flee to the woods. There, she met the prince, who was returning from a hunting trip. He asked her what she was doing alone in the forest.

The girl told him everything, emeralds and diamonds falling as she spoke.

The prince fell in love as they spoke and brought her to his castle to introduce her to his father. Considering the value of such a gift, the king agreed to their marriage. As for the rotten sister, she was so ashamed about her disgusting "gift" that she ran away and was never seen again.

Anna Lang

Anna Lang is a graphic designer and illustrator
who lives in Sardinia, Italy. She illustrated
her first book in 2015, and has illustrated many
other children's books since then.

STERLING CHILDREN'S BOOKS
New York

An Imprint of Sterling Publishing Co., Inc.
1166 Avenue of the Americas
New York, NY 10036

STERLING CHILDREN'S BOOKS and the distinctive Sterling Children's Books logo are registered
trademarks of Sterling Publishing Co., Inc.

ISBN 978-1-4549-4380-8

For information about custom editions, special sales, and premium and corporate purchases, please
contact Sterling Special Sales at 800-805-5489 or specialsales@sterlingpublishing.com.

Manufactured in Romania

Lot #:
2 4 6 8 10 9 7 5 3 1
08/21

sterlingpublishing.com

Design by Anna Lang
Illustrated by Anna Lang - Translation by Katherine Kirby